On the
Cold Coasts

On the Cold Coasts was first published in 2000 by Forlagid as *Galdur*. Translated from Icelandic by Alda Sigmundsdottir. Published in English by AmazonCrossing in 2012.

Published by AmazonCrossing
P.O. Box 400818
Las Vegas, NV 89140

ISBN-13: 9781611090956
ISBN-10: 1611090954
Library of Congress Control Number: 2011907088

On the Cold Coasts

Vilborg Davidsdottir
Translated by Alda Sigmundsdottir

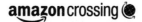

In memory of Juliana G.
1956–2000

Of Yselond to wryte is lytill nede,
Save of stokfische; yt for sothe in dede
Out of Bristow and costis may one,
Men have practised by needle and by stone
Thiderwardes wythine a lytel whylle,
Wythine xij. yere, and wythoute perille,
Gone and comen, as men were wont of olde
Of Scarborowg unto the costes colde;
And now so fele shippes thys yere there were.
That moche losse for unfraught they bare
Yselond myght not make hem to be fraught
Unto the hawys; this moche harme they caught.
—from "The Libelle of Englyshe Polycye," written around 1436

About Iceland, there is little need to write
Except for the stockfish; for indeed
These last twelve years, without peril
Voyages have been made, by needle and lodestone,
Thither out of Bristol and many another coastal town,
Back and forth in no time, as was the custom in the past,
From Scarborough to the cold coasts.
But now, this year, so many ships there were,
That they suffered great losses for lack of goods;
For Iceland could not produce enough
To make the voyage worthwhile: this much harm they had.

BITTER AS WORMWOOD

The girl on the bedstead screamed and clutched desperately at the older woman sitting next to her, as yet another contraction coursed through her body. Her blue-gray, bloodshot eyes widened horribly, like they would burst from their sockets. The midwife wiped streams of sweat from the girl's forehead with a linen cloth and brushed her straight, black hair to one side.

"Hush, child," she said wearily. "This hysteria will only make things harder."

Ragna Gautadottir made no reply. She barely heard what was being said anymore. She had been in labor since last night, and it was now past noon. Daylight had come and gone in a heartbeat, and twilight had once again descended on the snow-covered land. Outside was a cold and dark kingdom. It was the thirteenth day of January, the feast day of St. Hilary.

"In sorrow thou shalt bring forth children," said the Lord to Eve, "and thy desire shall be to thy husband." But there was no husband in the vicinity, and she who was enduring this sorrow was barely a woman herself.

The linen shift, soaked through with perspiration, clung to her body, clearly revealing the constriction of her taut belly during the contractions. Occasionally, in between, there was a billowing movement as the unborn child moved inside her. The child was impatient to see this world, unaware of all the toil and

1

trouble that awaited it, ignorant of all that was and would be. *Better if it had never been conceived, and best if it dies,* Ragna thought as she had a thousand times before, and instantly she felt ashamed of her thoughts. She stared up at the ceiling of the bedchamber and squinted to see better in the dim light of the lantern. She didn't have to—she knew precisely where it was. She had carved the letter in the rafter of the sloping ceiling above her bed: M for Michael. In her mind's eye, his boyish face appeared, pale and wan, as it had been that cursed day in April last year when she first saw him, dragged from the sea, weathered and beaten...

❦

They had all seemed dead at first, and no one was surprised. The blizzard that had started in the blink of an eye just before daybreak on Holy Thursday was over by noon. Even so, it was cold, and the men who lay scattered among the goods in the sand were drenched by the sea and the snow. Some of them looked asleep, the pallor of death on their skin the only indication that the Lord had already taken them into His merciful embrace. Others were so mutilated that a mere glance filled the onlooker with horror. Lying on the shore was a man with a leg bone protruding from his leather cloak, another with his head so askew that the neck was most certainly broken, and a third with eyes open and staring but only the whites visible and one of his arms all but torn from his body. His mouth was filled with sand, and a small snail crawled across his forehead. A flock of northern fulmars glided above, silently, as though out of respect for all this death; one had touched down on the back of a young boy's corpse and flew up with wings flapping as the group of people drew near. Despite the mutilation there was no blood; the corpses had already been washed in the salty water. Hel, the goddess of death, reigned here. There was an eerie quiet, no sound but the innocuous washing of the waves. A few eider ducks cooed softly at each other as they rode the waves between the land and the Helenarholmi islet. Three bodies lay on the raised beach, blue and dead in the wilted dune grass; most likely they had made it onto dry land alive, but had been given the kiss of death by the cold and their own injuries.

The rough, green waters of Skagafjord had sucked down two ships, lock, stock, and barrel. A third, the vessel *Trinity* of Bristol, had been driven up onto the black shore. The raging, white-capped waves had shattered the two-masted schooner and washed oak panels and cargo far up onto the land. The freight and supplies belonging to the English were scattered across the sands: shoes by the dozen, tin cups and plates, rolls of burlap, sailcloth and ropes, boxes and oars. A spared barrel of beer rolled back and forth on the shore with the movement of the waves.

It later transpired that two dozen English ships plus one had been wrecked off the shores of Iceland that very same morning, which in addition to being Holy Thursday was also the first day of summer according to the Icelandic calendar. Everyone on board perished, and the wrecked vessels and goods were driven up onto the various coastlines around the country.

All able-bodied folk were sent to the beach to collect the timber and other goods. The timber from the shipwreck was a treasure, and the people hurried to gather as much of the spoils as possible before the greedy waves licked the coastline clean once more. Tomorrow was Good Friday, and on that day no one was permitted to lift a finger, not even to save the precious wealth that the sea had yielded. Later that day, when twilight had begun to hamper visibility, the corpses were laid two and two across the horses that carried the lightest loads, and transported the shortest distance to the church of Vidvik. Along the way, one of the men surprised everyone by showing signs of life; seawater was regurgitated from the belly of a skinny, black-haired youth and ran down the side of the mare that carried him, down to the tussocked ground. He coughed violently and called out something in his native language.

On Saturday morning the seafarers, nearly thirty of them, were laid together in a single grave and a psalm was sung over them. The young man who had lived was taken to the bishopric at Holar in Hjaltadalur Valley, so the bishop, who was the most likely of the locals to know the odd word in English, could question him about the home ports of the ships that had perished, and ask news of England.

Many people were gathered at Holar on the Saturday before Easter. His Grace, Bishop Jon Tofason, had invited the elite of the see of Holar to celebrate the resurrection of the Savior, and the mass for consecrating the fire was about to commence when the youth was brought in. The fires had been extinguished in the hearths of all the farmhouses, and the folk were on their way to the cathedral to watch the bishop light and bless a new and pure Easter fire.

For that reason, the hapless and still badly disoriented seafarer was laid in a bed in the women's quarters. It was still unclear whether or not he would survive past Easter Sunday. Wenches dressed him in woolen undergarments, and a few children were made to get into bed with him to help warm him even more. Blankets and still more blankets were laid on top of them, so eventually they grew impossibly hot and sweaty. Very soon the children became restless and snuck from the bed one by one when the womenfolk had gone off to attend to more important tasks. All except one of the sisters from the Akrar estate, the older one, which malicious tongues liked to say had a hint of native Greenlandic blood—Skraeling blood—in her veins.

He had a tangle of seaweed in his tousled, shoulder-length hair, and he regained consciousness as Ragna was picking it out with deft fingers. It took some time, and while she did so she recited in a mellifluous voice the tale of Sassuma, Mother of the Greenland Sea, who sat on the ocean floor with seaweed in her great head of hair and drove away the hunters' prey unless the shaman came to comb out her tangles, braid her hair, and sing for her. "This is how they sing…" And she sang to him, disjointed tones in no-man's language: "*Qa-vam-mut kak-kak qii-ma-naq…*"

He did not understand a word of what she said, but he stared with ardent brown eyes at her dark-skinned countenance, and it calmed her to talk and to sing because just his gaze alone made her heart beat a little faster. His eyes shone, not from fever but from something entirely different. She remembered every line in his face, and how it lit up when he smiled, and every stroke of his hands, and the turbulence in her blood when he stroked her naked shoulders and belly and thighs. The pain she felt when he entered her took her by surprise but was instantly forgotten and of no consequence. He smiled and sighed with pleasure, and she felt his tongue in her mouth and sucked it greedily like a child sucks on its mother's breast, and she licked his chin, rough with stubble, and felt the salty taste of the fierce and frantic waves that had washed him up onto the beach.

◈

Ragna felt a contraction and grasped her head in her hands with a low, pitiful howl. It was like her body was being split open from her pelvis, through her spine, and up; her bones felt pried apart, her world ripped apart. The room swam before her eyes; someone was bending over her. Was it her mother?

"Mamma!" she screamed. "Help me!"

Sigridur Bjornsdottir, known as Sigridur the Rich, had been the first to comprehend her daughter's condition, although not until the end of summer when the weight had begun to show, and too late for any measures to be taken in secret. The girl, just fourteen winters old, had shown little understanding of what had happened, being completely ignorant of the natural and, indeed, deliberate consequences of the sensual acts performed by a man and a woman. This despite the fact that a year earlier she had been promised to a man in marriage, and the wedding was to take place as soon she turned fifteen and was fit to be wed. For that reason alone, Sigridur might already have informed her daughter of such consequences, remarked Ragna's foster-father Thorsteinn sternly, yet he made no allowance for this rather glaring omission when he decided Ragna's punishment. He gave her a good lashing with brushwood and made her fast on bread and water for seven days straight. Possibly he was hoping that the treatment might result in a miscarriage, and that was certainly her own fervent wish when she finally understood what it meant to be a fallen woman and a harlot.

Yet her sin was not only that of lying under that pathetic English dog outside of wedlock. Even more appalling was the fact that they had done the deed during Easter week, when intercourse between a man and a woman was strictly forbidden, as it was on all other holy days and most particularly when celebrating the resurrection of the Savior, when transgression meant heavy penance. She had defiled herself at a time when true, honest Christians did their utmost to cleanse the body and the soul through fasting and abstinence, and had thus put her own soul in peril.

Moreover, for this very reason it was considered highly likely that the child would be born deformed as an eternal reminder to its parent. Such could be the punishment of God Almighty if His Word was violated, Father Pall, the priest of Akrar, told her, his face flushed red with disapproval and indignation on behalf of the Lord, poking a long-nailed index finger into the girl's belly and causing her to retreat backward in alarm.

Even more painful was the humiliation when the two men from Muli in Adaldalur Valley came to Akrar to be given the news: Gudbjartur Floki and his son Thorkell, who a summer earlier had grinned at her with sincere anticipation as they shook hands to seal their engagement, and then kissed her once on each cheek, proud yet shy.

She was bathed and dressed in her best apparel prior to their arrival, a wide dress with short sleeves made of blue flax, gathered with a white belt beneath the breasts, though not tightly enough to make a bad situation seem worse. She wore a silver chain decorated with a small Holyrood around her neck and rings on her fingers. Her black, waist-length hair had been repeatedly washed and then combed so thoroughly that her scalp burned, bringing tears to her eyes. It was then braided and decorated with combs adorned with precious stones. Finally a line was drawn with charcoal across her arched brows and above her eyelashes to enhance her eyes, and her cheeks were pinched to make them rosy. After a sun-filled summer, her skin was already darker than usual, even though she had tortured herself daily by drinking dandelion tonic to make her complexion seem brighter. To no avail.

Thus primped and attired, she sat on the women's bench with her mother and younger sister, humble, with downcast eyes and glowing cheeks, when the men from Adaldalur Valley entered the parlor. She was rewarded with their admiring looks and warm greetings. The son was tall, already exceeding his father in height, with blond hair and dark, bushy eyebrows that gave him a particularly strong expression around the eyes, and long lashes like that of a woman. The childish look that had characterized his narrow face a year earlier had now vanished, and instead there was an ambiguous look about him, scrutinizing, yet so warm and penetrating that Ragna grew shy and disconcerted and utterly timid.

But all fondness disappeared from their faces when Lawman Thorsteinn gave a long-winded explanation filled with digressions about the current and particular situation of the subject. No sympathy was spared for her even though he took it upon himself to include in the story that the miscreant, who had abandoned the scene on a sailing vessel before the discovery was made, had forced the girl's will through violence. Thorkell gave Ragna a distraught and disbelieving look, and she wanted nothing more than to disappear down through the floor, consumed by her own shame, not daring to raise her eyes.

After much hemming, hawing, coughing, and spitting, Gudbjartur Floki finally spoke. Despite this sudden and unfortunate matter, he said, he did not wish to automatically terminate their earlier agreement, though obviously circumstances were very much altered and called for compensation in the form of land and livestock, for everyone understood the damage to the reputation of all those concerned.

Ragna sat silently while they bickered about land and live-stock and her. She stared into the crackling fire in the hearth and in her mind recited bits of a rhyme that her nurse had sang to her when she was a child, hoping to calm herself and block out what was being said, but alas, without success. In the end she could take no more; she stood up and left the room without a word. Her mother went after her and took hold of her shoulder, but Ragna tore herself loose and Sigridur let her be.

She sought refuge next to the large haystack to the west of the barn, sat down with her legs extended, and began to weep. As it was the Lord's day of rest, there was no one about, yet a moment later, a shadow fell on her.

"Thorsteinn has offered a decent patch of land in Greenland with you and the bairn, but he's only willing to part with Litla-Grund here at home, even though he's a major landowner, with a dozen pieces all told."

She was startled and looked up, teary-eyed, to see her intend-ed, Thorkell Gudbjartsson, towering above her, long-legged in tight breeches and long-toed shoes with curved pikes. His golden hair with its tight waves radiated in the sunshine. He had a deep voice. "Seems your stepfather is no longer so keen to marry you off, Ragna. Unless he would prefer us to pick up and move to the Eastern Settlement in Greenland."

She made no reply and looked away to hide the redness in her eyes; she looked straight ahead. It felt uncomfortable to have him so near, and above her. Thorkell sat down on his haunches next to her and leaned his back against the haystack. He rested his elbows on his knees, put a hand under one cheek, and looked at her with those ambiguous eyes. In her range of vision were his thighs and calves; she could see that they were strong and muscular.

"What would you think of that, young miss, seeing as you were born and raised in that faraway hinterland, or do you not remember that time?" He pulled up a straw, stuck it in his mouth, and chewed, arrogant and carefree. He seemed to not give a hoot that at that very moment there were deals being made with both of their lives in the main parlor, schemes and negotiations about what should become of the two of them.

Clouds alternately merged and separated in the sky above Blonduhlid. She gazed at them and tried to make it seem as though she cared as little as he did.

"The Eastern Settlement of Greenland is not a hinterland," she finally said softly, and sniffled. "And anyway, what does it matter what I think about anything?"

"Stop sniffling," he said with a hint of compassion and pulled a small kerchief from his sleeve for her to blow her nose; he came from a good family. "I'll get a better piece of land out of the deal, and it will all work out."

Ragna took the kerchief; it was made of linen and laced with fine blue embroidery, with his monogram stitched in one corner. Carefully she dried her eyes and nose. In a large chest inside the house, she had a grand collection of fine textiles: bedding and tablecloths woven with golden threads, and wall tapestries, many ells in length, all marked with their initials, and in Roman letters the symbol of the coming year, their wedding year, with sprays and leaves and blossoms in all colors embroidered around them. All those stitches, each infused with her dreams and eagerness to become her own mistress on her own farm. Most likely they had all been for naught and would come to nothing. All of it was unraveling before her eyes, and it was her own fault. Ragna wanted to start weeping again but collected herself and handed Thorkell back his kerchief, grimy from the charcoal that had been used on her eyes.

The child in her belly kicked and thrashed. It might even be turning somersaults in her womb. She couldn't help herself—she liked the feeling. She put her hand on the spot where the movement had been, for suddenly it reminded her that, at the very least, the two of them had each other, no matter how everything else turned out. That touched her deeply, even though this very same life was to blame for how everything had turned out. How could one hate and love a tiny thing that wasn't even a person yet, both at the same time? She sighed, almost inaudibly.

"Is it moving?" He wasn't pompous anymore. His deep voice was almost reverent.

She nodded, and felt a childlike pride that at least she was capable of finding a life stirring inside of her.

"Do you want to feel?" she asked, surprising even herself. Hesitantly he extended a long-fingered hand, and she placed it tightly on her belly, holding her own over his. "This is where it kicks the most."

The baby was quite still now, almost as though it was teasing them. Not even so much as a butterfly fluttering in her uterus. They waited, quietly. She smiled, feeling awkward. Finally came a strong and decisive kick. Thorkell laughed, surprised, when he felt it against his palm. "What a strong fellow," he said, as though it had to be a boy. Ragna felt slightly more hopeful; perhaps all would be well after all. He did not withdraw his hand, and she let hers continue lying over his. Thus they sat, quiet and still, except that Thorkell moved his thumb back and forth a little bit, and those movements awakened in her strange impulses that were almost certainly not appropriate, even though they were, theoretically, betrothed.

A short while later, Gudbjartur Floki called brusquely to his son that they were leaving; they would not be spending the night at Akrar, and had a long journey ahead of them.

"Will you allow me a kiss?"

She turned her cheek toward him but found to her surprise his cool lips touching her neck, just beneath her ear, and heard him inhale deeply. "You smell so good," he said.

Then they left.

❖

The arrival of the English had been welcomed at first, since ships from Norway had become a rare sight and for a long time there had been a shortage of numerous commodities. The Icelanders sold stockfish to the English and received in return flour and honey, soap and pewter, English linen and shoes made of cowhide. Thorsteinn of Akrar had prospered in his dealings with the English, being one of the first to establish connections with them in the north. But the novelty soon wore off and disputes about pricing began. The English acted as if they alone could decide how much should be paid for the fish, and were moreover beginning to fish themselves from their vessels and barks, using tremendously long lines with dozens of hooks on each one. They salted the catch instead of filling their holds only with Icelandic stockfish. Usually the ribalds sailed away in the fall on ships loaded with fish for which they had not paid a tariff to the king of Norway and Iceland, or even the correct price. Lately conflicts had arisen between the foreigners and the locals with increasing frequency, to the point where blows were exchanged. It was said that Gudbjartur Floki of Muli and his son Thorkell had been involved in a dispute with the captain of *Trinity* of Bristol, and some thought it uncanny how suddenly the storm had begun on the morning of Holy Thursday; in the blink of an eye, it had changed from a light breeze to a heavy blizzard with winds from the north. Gudbjartur Floki had long been notorious for dabbling in the dark arts, what people referred to as *galdur*. "Apparently the son also knows a thing or two about sorcery and such matters, and in any case, he was not suited to you," Sigridur told her daughter and stroked her cheek. She omitted to mention the obvious fact that a year earlier both she and her husband had been rather in favor of forging a strong bond with those wealthy and ambitious men from Muli. There would be other suitors and of a better ilk, she said, and in any event the inheritance was plentiful and there was still time, at least for a while. The men from Muli could keep their arrogant ways and their own company. It was said that Thorkell himself had fathered two bastard children with his father's wenches, and the woman who would marry him would never have him to herself. Besides, he was said to be quick-tempered and with a difficult disposition.

The mistress of Akrar shook her auburn hair and whispered these and similar words of comfort to her daughter when her husband was out of earshot. It was not even certain that the child would live; in fact, it was just as likely that it would die. Who knew better than she about such things, who had been with child ten times but had only two daughters alive, Ragna and little Kristin, who had just turned seven. Two miscarriages; four children had passed before they could walk, all from sickness of the lungs; and the first and last had been stillborn. Those two had not been christened, but her firstborn, who had never drawn the breath of life, a tiny boy with a crop of dark hair and balled fists, had been buried in consecrated earth. The Greenlanders were not as heartless as the Icelanders, who refused to allow those who were not christened to be buried in a churchyard, just like they did with those who took their own lives. They would never rest in peace. He was buried beneath the wall of the church of Hvalsey in Greenland, next to his father, brother, and three sisters, the same church in which Sigridur had been given in marriage to Thorsteinn Olafsson twelve years before.

◆

At long last it seemed as if the red pebble of relief was starting to work its magic and ease the birthing, though not until the midwife had also bound a vellum leaf from *Vita of St. Margaret* to the girl's thigh. With joint effort the women were able to get her onto the floor when the contractions came with increasing frequency, and then the pushing began. Ragna was barely able to stand and fell, heavy and exhausted, onto her knees, like a helpless beached whale. Her mother crossed herself when she saw the thick rivulets of blood that streamed down the girl's thighs. A maroon-colored puddle formed on the wooden floor, and the pungent smell of iron filled the air.

"Holy Mary, Mother of God, help us," Sigridur moaned, distraught, knowing that the worst thing of all had happened: the girl was torn on the inside and the baby was not out yet. From the corner of her eye, she saw the angel of death standing in the dusky corner of the room with that familiar look of sorrow. Ragna screamed with renewed energy and pain, and a head with black hair appeared between her legs. One shoulder emerged, and then the other, the child so broad-shouldered and large that the two women had never seen anything like it; surely this was the Lord's penalty for fornication during Easter. The same instant as her son slid into this world in a torrent of blood, darkness bestowed its mercy on Ragna, and everything vanished.

The midwife recited all the incantations that she knew for stopping blood flow in a singsong voice, burning incense all the while. "Cease blood red that I see flowing, blood burning, blood turning, blood halting, the flood halted when the Savior died, hold back thy blood of death..."

Yet although the incantations worked and the flow of blood from the uterus slowed and finally stopped completely, it seemed clear that Ragna would not live. No one could lose so much blood and still survive. Father Pall anointed her and gave her the final sacrament while there was still a tiny fluttering spirit within her chest; it was safest that way.

Her mother spent the entire night on her knees in the church and prayed, adjured blessed Margaret, blessed Thorlak, blessed Mary, Mother of God, yes all the saints with churches throughout north Iceland, to let her daughter live. In Sigridur Bjornsdottir's forty winters on this earth, the angel of death had followed her every step. It had snatched one infant after another away from her during the fifteen years that she had lived in Greenland, and when the Great Plague raged in Iceland, her immediate family was all afflicted. Her parents and siblings coughed up blood and gave up the ghost within a few days. She was the only survivor from the lineage of Bjorn the Rich Brynjolfsson from Akrar in Blonduhlid, and she had not even known about her bereavement and related wealth until two years later when Thorsteinn came from Iceland bearing news of all the land, tenants, and livestock that now belonged to her alone. In addition to Thorleiksstadir, Mosagrund, and Vaglar, which had been her dowry at the age of fifteen, she was now the owner of the Akrar lands, as well as the farms of Brekkur, Grof, Gegnisholl, Vellir, Reykir on

Reykjastrond, Dadastadir, both of the Grund lands, and four sections of land in Laxardalur Valley. Of course she alone now also bore all the obligations and taxes that accompanied this vast inheritance, as well as responsibility for the livestock and tenant farmers.

The previous spring God had given her Ragna, who was born healthy and likely to live. In the fall, He had taken Gauti from her. He fell overboard during the seal hunt, and although they managed to pull him from the icy Hvalseyjarfjord just moments later, it was already too late—the brutal frost had reached his heart and it had ceased beating.

"Haven't you taken enough?" Sigridur cried out to the crucified Christ on the altarpiece and lit one wax candle after another with trembling hands for each loved one that He taken from her, until the church was fully illuminated. Surely He could see in that divine light that she had been punished enough, whatever she had done to deserve it. "Take the boy, but let my Ragna live and forgive my selfishness," she whispered and clasped her hands together so tightly that the knuckles turned white, praying unceasingly in this manner until daybreak. "I shall endure anything, anything at all, if only you let my daughter live."

Whether due to Sigridur's fervent prayers or the midwife's incantations, the Lord showed mercy and allowed both to live, Ragna and the boy. Not only that, but the girl recovered astonishingly quickly. The midwife announced, however, that the new mother would scarcely survive something like that for a second time. She was so badly maimed from giving birth to her eleven-pound son that another birth would most certainly kill her.

The girl named the boy after his father, who had sailed away across the sea. She let them decide everything else, but on this she would not budge, surprising herself as much as those closest to her with her own stubbornness. "Michael, like the archangel," said Sigridur, when asked where the name had come from. Yet most of the people in the district guessed the truth and chuckled to themselves with satisfaction that the uppity folks at Akrar had received due penance for their own self-importance. It served them well to be brought down a notch, what with Thorsteinn being given the post of lawman, and by Jove if he didn't covet the office of governor of the Norwegian king as well.

◇

"According to the Apostle Paul, he who sins must be punished before the entire congregation to invoke fear in others," said His Grace, Bishop Jon Tofason, sternly. He made the remark when it became clear to him that the husband and wife of Akrar would not follow his advice and place Ragna in the custody of Thorunn, prioress of the Reynistadur convent, and along with her those worldly goods that were her rightful paternal inheritance—specifically Hvalsey, a highly prosperous tract of land in the Eastern Settlement of Greenland.

Normally only major sinners such as fornicators and criminals were made to suffer public indulgence, but the bishop would not budge from his decision. This even though Sigridur argued that her daughter had been taken by force and was moreover ignorant of her sins due to her young age and lack of maturity. She asked that her churching take place at the Akrar church. Ragna, however, dashed her mother's hopes in that regard when the bishop asked if the seafarer had forced her into intercourse. She dared not tell a lie; her list of sins was long and severe enough as it was. And so she told the truth: that she had willingly lain with the youth, adding that it had given her pleasure, which was the final straw in the mind of His Grace Jon Tofason.

The churching took place exactly forty days after Michael's birth, and it fell upon the feast day of Saint Peter during Great Lent. There were many people in attendance in Holar cathedral, even more than might be expected at the freezing cold and windy beginning of Goa, the third month according to the Icelandic calendar, in late February. The ground was pale with a thin veil of snow, and there was the occasional snowdrift, though not enough to stop churchgoers from joining in the procession around the church before the service. The snow crunched beneath the feet of the congregation, an icy fog hovered around the muzzles of the horses in the cold, and massive icicles hung from the tin roof of the cathedral.

Ragna waited near the church doors after the people had entered, as was common practice. To her relief she noted that she was not the only one to be churched that day. Alongside her waited Gudridur Aladottir from Thufnakot, who had given birth to her eighth child shortly before the Feast of Saint Paul. Her worn garments attested to her poverty, but she bore a headdress denoting her status as a married woman and in that respect was more finely dressed than Ragna, who ran a trembling hand through her long, uncut maiden's hair. She had nothing covering her head but her shawl, and it made her feel naked. In the chill of the dusky narthex, she pulled it more tightly across herself and the infant boy. He was sound asleep, while Gudridur's girl whimpered weakly on her arm, no matter how much the mother shushed and rocked her.

The acolyte boy came over to them with a lighted candle and handed it to the older woman. Then the prayers of mercy—Kyrie Eleison and Christe Eleison—were sung repeatedly. Next came the long *collectio* prayer, after which Father Jon Palsson, priest and *officialis in spiritualibus*, stout and with his chest slightly thrust forward, came to the narthex where they were standing. He sprinkled holy water from the baptismal font over both of them and on the children while mumbling a prayer. That done, he placed his hand on Gudridur's arm and led her slowly down the aisle so the wax from the candle that she gripped tightly in her hand would not drip on her. Ragna remained behind, unsure of what to do, presuming that the acolyte would bring a candle for her after the ministers and congregation had got down on their knees and prayed for Gudridur's infant. The boy did come to her after the prayer, but without the candle, and he whispered for her to walk to the altar. The girl uttered her disbelief. Was she to enter alone with her son in her arms without the light of the Lord to guide her through the darkness cast by her sins? He nodded and made a sign for her to start walking, but she just stood there, her legs refusing to obey, her knees trembling from all those harsh looks that were directed her way, some of them filled with curiosity, others full of indignation, and many showing scarcely concealed pleasure and malice.

Michael woke and looked up at her with big eyes that had already begun to turn brown. His little mouth curved slightly and he gave her his first smile, and she smiled back at this little imp who could rely on no one but her. She no longer felt paralyzed. She walked quickly down the aisle and kept her head high. People turned as she passed, and those sitting on the floor at the outer edges of the rows on each side moved slightly aside, or she might just have stepped on someone's toes, as if by accident. Dozens of candles in tall, gilded holders cast a flickering light over the entire nave and on the red sandstone floor that seemed to reflect back a dark red shadow on the congregation.

Father Jon Palsson was waiting for her at the altar. As before, he recited the obligatory blessing over the infant, accompanied by the congregation. The bishop, who had his back turned to them, was bowed in prayer on a kneeler before Christ on the cross. He stood up and approached her, extending a book made of vellum. "Confess thy sins thus," he said.

She peered at the letters and read the words slowly and hesitantly, almost stuttering, in such a weak voice that it could barely be heard beyond the front rows: "I, sinful woman, willingly give myself over to God almighty and Our Lady Saint Mary for my manifold sins, for I have violated the Word of my Creator by..." Michael had begun to grow heavy in her arms, and as she tried to lift him, he wailed loudly so that it echoed from the dome over the high altar. No one except perhaps the bishop could hear the words that followed, irrespective of how people strained forward and cupped their ears in their hands. Jon Palsson awkwardly took Michael from her and handed him to the deacon, who nearly dropped the boy and was visibly relieved when Sigridur Bjornsdottir bustled forth to take her grandson in her arms. Michael's wailing stopped as quickly as it had begun, just as his mother completed her recitation: "...*in nomine Patris, et Filii, et Spiritus Sancti. Amen.*"

But it was not yet over. Her true penitence must be demonstrated in practice, and she was instructed to lie facedown on the stone slabs with her arms extended in humility before the Lord. The bishop then sang the indulgence over her to release her from the bondage of sin, in the name of the Holy Father and blessed Apostles and Holy Mother, the church. The floor was cold, and dust and incense filled her nostrils, and as she lay there prostrate with her eyes closed, she wondered yet again why God had not simply taken her life when she gave birth to Michael, instead of forcing her to endure such humiliation.

Yet her penitence, in the end, was not terribly severe: over the next year she was to recite the Lord's Prayer, genuflecting three times morning and night, thus securing mercy from the Lord above. That being decreed, she was at last permitted to get to her feet and take a seat on a chair next to her mother and sister, and the service could continue.

The deacon intoned the sermon and the gospel, and the members of the congregation took their eyes off the girl, for even though God's Word was read in church Latin and was incomprehensible to the unlettered, it was shown the proper respect, and the churchgoers gazed at the floor while it was being read. The sneaking glances resumed when the sermon began, and His Grace the bishop focused on the wisdom of King Solomon: "*For the lips of a strange woman drop as an honeycomb, and her mouth is smoother than oil: But in the end she is bitter as wormwood, sharp as a two-edged sword. Her feet go down to death; her steps take hold on hell....*"

Ragna turned her gaze from all of them and directed it at the side altar in the northern transept, where a dark-complexioned and blue-eyed Mary sat on a glittering throne with her young son swathed in her arms. Through her mind rushed a strange and almost blasphemous thought: the Queen of Heaven herself had been a fourteen-year-old unmarried girl when she gave birth to her firstborn child, who was not conceived with her betrothed. A comforting smile appeared and then just as suddenly vanished from the icon's face, and Ragna Gautadottir knew in her heart, whatever were the thoughts of the parish folk, that she was not condemned by the Mother of God.

THE GOODWILL OF CHIEFTAINS

―――――――――― ▬ ――――――――――

A few years after the night of the many shipwrecks, the English set up a small trading post near the mouth of the Kolbeinsa River, not far from the place where the *Trinity* of Bristol had been stranded. Buildings were raised out of turf and stone in the local manner, and hovels and storehouses were built for keeping stockfish. The people of Skagafjord kept quiet about the proceedings; many of them had commercial ties to the English, providing them with water and provisions from spring until fall, in return for generous compensation in goods.

For a time there was no bishop at the Holar bishopric following the death of the Danish Jon Tofason, which led to much conflict and debate over a substitute and successor. Thorsteinn of Akrar, lawman of North and West Iceland, took it upon himself to protect the interests of Holar in dealings with foreign traders, collecting the king's tariffs from the English. Men visited him from far and wide to haggle over stockfish and land and goodness knew what else.

As it happened, Thorsteinn operated his own ship, albeit in secret. Henry V, king of England, and his brother-in-law Eric of Pomerania, king of Denmark and Norway, had sealed an agreement that forbade anyone other than Eric's subjects to trade with the Icelanders. Ambitious businessmen and seafarers in England paid little heed to the embargo, especially since Eric had no way of enforcing it. He had his work cut out back home, fighting against the increasingly greedy merchants of the Hanseatic League and their pirate ships, and others that harried the seas like never before. Yet the king would surely not turn a blind eye were it to be heard at court that the lawman of Iceland himself was operating a vessel to England, and the office would be at risk. Thorsteinn's ship, *Christopher* of Hull, was therefore registered to an English vessel operator and had an English crew, with the sole exception of the captain. His name was Klaengur, a red-bearded Viking who had sailed Thorsteinn's ship for years on his voyages to Greenland and Norway, a cheerful man who had the ocean waves surging through his blood.

Michael, son of Ragna, followed Klaengur's every step each time he visited Akrar, curious and inquisitive, doing his utmost to win his favor. He had decided that he would take over as captain of the *Christopher* as soon as he was old enough, and he nagged until he had persuaded the English lads to show him the right moves when it came to working the fishing lines and trawls. Occasionally the crew would stay at Akrar, and the boy would not leave them in peace, even though a few of the sailors would frequently clip his ear or flick their finger at him when they felt he was getting in their way. Yet most of them were kindly, and the first mate even showed him a treasure that he claimed to be of more value to those who sail the open seas than all other things: the astrolabe, a disc-shaped wonder made of brass that showed the position of a ship out at sea even when there was no land in sight. It was not very large, with a diameter of just seven inches, but it was relatively heavy and had an adjustable dial that was set according to the position of the sun at noon, or the North Star at midnight. The face had an imprint of symbols signifying the planets in the sky and rings that showed their movements according to the seasons. The boy examined the disc from all sides, beside himself with admiration, and in no time he had made sense of how it worked and learned to use the relevant terminology, in both Nordic and English.

Klaengur the Red smiled at Michael's enthusiasm and remarked to the lawman that it might be a good idea to take the boy along on the next voyage; it might cool his sailor's blood to have to wrangle with the rough seas off Greenland. Thorsteinn thought it not such a bad idea, but he made no reply. The shame that Ragna had brought upon the family a decade earlier was no longer his greatest concern, even though that humiliation was by no means forgotten, neither by himself nor his adversaries in the ever-hardening battle over wealth and trade in North Iceland.

The leader of that faction was now Thorkell Gudbjartsson, who following the termination of his betrothal to Ragna had voyaged to France where he had studied theology for three winters. He was evidently just as partial to temporal as to spiritual riches, and he had not entirely rejected the pleasures of the flesh despite his newly taken vows, for there were rumors of yet another bastard child in addition to the two he was to have fathered prior to his overseas sojourn. And now this man, whom Thorsteinn had once intended to make a part of his family, had become steward, *officialis in temporalibus*, at Holar. That made him next in line to Father Jon Palsson, who had been *officialis* in spiritual matters at the bishopric for years, a deputy and executor of power in the absence of the newly appointed bishop, who was still abroad. These hieratic rulers had terminated all agreements with the lawman concerning the sale of stockfish for Holar and its properties. Instead, Thorkell was now responsible for all trade and collecting of tolls and tithes for the diocese, and he showed no leniency to those who were tardy with their payments. It was a mystery to the lawman how Thorkell had come so far in such a short time, being barely thirty winters old. Power and wealth were drawn to him like flies to a flame. The rumors were probably true: that he had learned a thing or two at the Black School of the Dark Arts— that served him well, and not only in the clergy.

What a miserable fool I was to think that Thorkell would forgive my youth, to hope he would rush the wedding for my sake and take the child as his own. Instead, he chose to humiliate me. He had a choice—but what choice did I have? None. I was forced to prostrate myself on the cold stone floor in Holar cathedral in front of the commoners and my own people, the priest and bishop, and disgrace myself, crying out for forgiveness for a sin that I scarcely understood until long after it was committed. Such an innocent I was. Until that day I was led to believe that I was worth something, that I had rights, and that I was allowed hopes and dreams. But not since. Even my mother, who protected and defended me at the outset, has grown distant and is gradually disappearing into Thorsteinn's shadow.

My stepfather prefers to keep the land intact, here as in Greenland, since the tenants pay the rent in the increasingly valuable stockfish. Would that be the reason that I am still here at home, unmarried, while my sister Kristin has been given to a man in marriage? Are my people aware that my life is in danger if I give birth to another child? Would the midwife speak of such a thing? Hardly.

How long did I entertain hope, foolish child that I was, that my Michael would return and take me away on his ship to a foreign land, where there were castles and other adventures to behold, another life where I could stand tall and look people in the eye. I had to have hope. I allowed them to bend me, but not to break me.

Despite all this, I am aware that my life is better in many ways than that of others who have succumbed to the same sin: lust for a man who is not their husband. I have heard of women who have been cast out, who wander from farm to farm and live on charity, who have lost everything along with their treasured virginity. Their children have been taken from them, as well as their honor and their future, and even their very lives. So should I then concur with those who judge me, who judge us all and refuse us access to the society of the just? Why is Thorkell not judged for his bastard children and the women he has betrayed? Why is he able to look others in the eye and amass power and wealth and the goodwill of the chieftains? Why him and not me? I want to shout these and other questions at their indignant glances, cast them before all those judges, demand answers, if not peacefully then violently. But I know it is no use, for this is how it has been arranged. So efficiently arranged. Of what consequence is one fallen woman, whether her family is powerful or not? I thirst for some kind of justice, something to call my own.

Though I know not what.

◇

A crowd had gathered on the beach at the mouth of the Kolbeinsa River. The ship carrying the new bishop had lowered its sails and dropped its anchor a short distance from Helenarholmi. A handful of cloudlets drifted through the clear blue sky, the heavy scent of late summer hung in the air, and the grass rippled like green waves in the fields. The sea was smooth and glittered in the sun, green-hued from the sea vegetation near the shore, dusky blue further out, near Drangey Island and Thordarhofdi. Malmey Island hovered on the horizon like a distant and unexplored wonderland in the mist. Waves rolled gently in and out, their lace borders white and vivid on the black sand. Fat bluebottles buzzed all around, contented from the nearby plenitude in the stockfish stores of the English.

Michael pulled away from his mother and ran to the shore to see what he could see. The bishop's ship was a large balinger, a speedy and splendiferous vessel with a castle in bow and stern, rigged with three lateen sails. Its name and home port were painted on the black bow in large, red letters: *Leonard de London*. The crew was still landing the cargo, mostly flour and malt casks and barrels filled with precious salt; they ferried this on a small dinghy from ship to land and stacked it all up on the raised beach, a safe distance from the incoming tide. Also among their cargo were an abundance of chests, some made out of rough wooden panels and of lesser quality, others finer and locked, ornately decorated and lined with silver, undoubtedly belonging to the man who was now clambering down a rope ladder to the dinghy. Seabirds glided above him, screeching on their way to the shore, caring nothing for office or title, having learned the one thing that mattered: that where there is a ship, there is a chance of food. Within a short time, the boat had reached the shore, and the new spiritual, and in some respects the temporal, authority of North Iceland was on dry land after weeks of tossing about on the Atlantic Ocean. This was His Grace John Williamsson Craxton from England, whom Pope Martin V had appointed bishop of Holar in Hjaltadalur Valley.

The dinghy was rowed to the ship once more to fetch more passengers, as the bishop had taken along with him a sympatric entourage.

The gaping boy watched from a distance as his grandfather Thorsteinn went before all the rest to receive the bishop. The two men greeted each other cordially. Craxton was a tall and wiry man, wore no beard in the priestly tradition, had a dark rim of hair around his shaved crown, and small, darting eyes that seemed to take in everything at once. His garments were impressive: a maroon cloak, trimmed with fur, and high leather boots. On his head he wore a chaperon with a long liripipe extending down the back. The boy thought Thorsteinn's apparel no less impressive: the lawman wore an otter coat slung over his shoulders, and underneath a striped, button-down velvet singlet and tight, dark-green breeches. The women of Akrar—Sigridur and her daughters—were elaborately attired with white wimples made of silk, clad in many-layered dresses and coats made of velvet and trimmed with scarlet, so that all who looked on could see that these were persons of consequence. Michael inadvertently straightened his back and pushed his own chaperon back on his head; he had a tendency to carry himself slightly stooped in an unconscious attempt to downplay his height and broad shoulders, so uncommon for his young age.

The bishop greeted people to the left and right, and Michael watched eagerly as Thorsteinn turned his attention to Ragna and presented her. She collected her skirts in her left hand and curtsied deeply, and with her right she took the bishop's extended hand and kissed his ring. That same moment a large man came walking toward them, with sharp eyes, a bare face, and flaxen hair. He was clearly a priest, judging by his crown and attire, and Ragna retreated away from him so quickly that she nearly fell. The boy watched his mother's expression change from fear to anger to shame in an instant, and he was filled with a sudden and inexplicable fury. Impulsively, as was his wont, he ran to the front of the crowd to stand next to her. Without knowing how it happened, he slipped at the same moment as he reached his mother, almost as if someone had tripped him. He grasped at the air as he fell, his hand finding red fabric that gave way and tore along a seam, and then he was lying flat in the sand in front of all those people, gasping from the humiliation and also the tremendous blow he had taken to the solar plexus when he fell on a rock. The flaxen-haired man reached down, took hold of one of his ears, and pulled him to his feet.

"How dare you disgrace the bishop, idiot boy!" he said derisively, shaking Michael so that he thought his ear would be torn clean away from his head. From the corner of his eye, he saw his mother color crimson, and the expression on Thorsteinn's face made him wish he had wings like his namesake, the archangel.

"Let the boy go, Thorkell," said Thorsteinn coldly. The ear was released, and Michael felt himself shoved to one side. Ragna pulled him close. She said nothing, just held her arm tightly around his shoulders.

"Mr. Craxton, my grandson Michael," Thorsteinn said, and a narrow smile forced its way onto his lips as he gestured in the boy's direction. "I ask Your Grace to kindly forgive this unhappy incident. The boy is impulsive and lacks refinement."

The bishop's stone-gray eyes met Michael's brown ones. The boy tried to return the gaze with his head held high, but his cheeks burned from the bishop's stinging gaze, and to his despair he found that his eyes were beginning to water. Craxton's expression grew milder. He smiled, revealing large, yellow teeth. He patted the boy awkwardly on the shoulder, at the same time touching Ragna's milky white hand, as if by chance.

"It is only natural for young lads to be energetic," he said, speaking slowly and with a foreign accent, though he was easily understood. "If his mother is willing to have my cloak sewn, we shall call it even."

Ragna curtsied and gave Michael a poke. He bowed down as far toward the sand as he could, and an audible sigh of relief passed through the crowd. A moment later people had begun to chat as though nothing unusual had taken place. Michael had planned to sneak away to get a better look at the bishop's ship, the three masts so amazingly tall that it would take a true hero to climb up to the highest rigging without catching vertigo, but his mother refused to let go of his hand. To his relief, however, she said nothing about the unfortunate event. She rarely scolded him, in any case; she treated him more like a friend than as a child. If he was to be punished for misbehaving, she usually got him off, and she never hit him. Thorsteinn mostly ignored him, and his aunt Kristin—who was only seven winters older than he—was kind to him and even spoiled him a little. Thus he had more freedom than many children of the same age and could come and go as he pleased without anyone chiding him for it, so long as he carried out those few chores that he was assigned. He was taller than most of his peers and fought with knuckles and fists against anyone who dared tease him about the absence of his father.

"My father is an important sea captain in England," he boasted to anyone who would listen. Except of course the people back home, at Akrar. There was not much talk of this there, and indeed many things were not spoken of.

For the most part, it was his grandmother Sigridur who disciplined him, but she, too, took pity on him when something was amiss. Perhaps there was something about the boy that reminded her of her sons who were buried in Greenland. He could just as well have inherited his dark appearance from Gauti, who had

had Skraelings among his forebears, as from his father, that hapless Englishman.

Immediately on his arrival in Iceland, it became evident that John Craxton did not lag behind his countrymen when it came to trade. He produced a signed permit from King Henry V authorizing him to import flour and malt and to send his ship back to England loaded with stockfish from the Holar stores. Before long the bishop had taken full control of Holar. He began putting in order various matters that had been allowed to slip in the years when the diocese had been without a bishop and was governed by leaders of varying competence in both worldly and spiritual affairs. He made a point of having good relations with anyone who mattered. That summer he paid visits to chieftains throughout North Iceland and was generous with the malt. In other words, he was a clever ruler and a lackey to no man. One by one he dismissed those men who had been appointed during the reign of his Danish predecessor, whom he considered to be a little too partial to King Eric and at the same time opposed to the influx of the English. That included Father Jon Palsson, who had made no secret of his loyalty toward the archbishop in Nidaros and, indeed, had visited him there several years earlier. No one could therefore doubt that beneath the bishop's adornments beat an English heart, despite Craxton's maternal lineage being Nordic.

The bishop rode into the farmyard at Akrar with a dozen men on a calm fall day, shortly after the slaughter season. The sky was nearly clear, though spotted with wispy white clouds, the sun hanging low in the sky. It was cold and the shoes of the horses clattered on the frozen ground. The general appearance of the entourage suggested that a person of influence was among them. The men were well attired, their capes and hats trimmed with fur, their boots high on the leg, and their tight hose colorful. They had English ale to drink, spoke loudly, and laughed easily. The bishop presented the lawman with a keg of hops as a gift, to have mead brewed for his church. After mass they sat down to a feast where food and drink were presented in abundance. The mistress and her two daughters served at the high table; maidservants waited on those of lower rank.

Thus Ragna could not escape the looks of her former betrothed, Thorkell Gudbjartsson, yet this time she did not flinch and returned his gaze, seemingly without fear, though her heart was beating wildly in her chest. His dusky blue eyes studied her, cold at first, but his gaze seemed to grow softer when she did not look away, changing from arrogance to something like curiosity. She poured drinks for him and served his food, smiling and warm, unlike herself, making her movements intentionally fluid so that her body would reflect the softness within. She would not allow Thorkell to see her bitter and harsh from his betrayal; instead, she would make him regret his rejection and long for that which was no longer available to him.

His Grace the bishop also kept her within his line of vision, kind and polite, thanking her for all the food that she served them, holding forth at length about the Icelanders' hospitality and generosity. He spoke frequently of the school at Holar that he planned to resurrect and where he intended to teach the sons of chieftains. A rector had already been appointed, and a number of boys fourteen and fifteen winters old were already on site, but there was still room for more, and what did the lawman think about sending the boy Michael to be educated at Holar, for his own benefit and as an example to others?

Thorsteinn thought it over. "That is indeed a generous offer, but the boy is a mere eleven winters old," he finally replied, "three to four winters younger than the other lads in the school. Is that not a bit too young, his precociousness notwithstanding?"

"His mother could accompany him," suggested Bishop Craxton, coming now to his real business with the lawman. The Holar bishopric, he said, had long suffered from the absence of a capable woman to set things in order and to supervise the female servants. The butler supervised the pantry and kitchen, but he could not fully manage things in the hall. Moreover, a servant had recently absconded from service after accusing the butler of harsh treatment. He was therefore in a tight spot, since there was a lack of servants in the country following the great plague, which had wiped out a large portion of the nation a mere two and a half decades earlier. Indeed, the labor shortage was such that even criminals who had completed their sentences could have their pick of employment.

"The lawman would do me a great favor and I would be deeply indebted if he would lend me a housekeeper. Providing, of course, that the young lady is in agreement," he said and extended his hands with palms raised, pleading and humble, the great man of God.

⟨⟡⟩

A housekeeper at Holar in Hjaltadalur Valley. Managing other servants. Overseeing the bishop's feasts. Being somebody. Is this for real? All eyes are on me. Yes! Say yes! Release me from this place.

No sound escaped my lips. Only an innocuous smile, an amiable manner. All on the surface.

My stepfather looks to my mother; a slight nod in agreement. It could be useful for him to have me at Holar. It is a sure way to gain reliable news, quickly. And the bishop would be in their debt. Yes, why not?

But what of my Michael? Will Thorkell make him pay for his mother's sins?

Men devise their schemes. They hold all the power. Women simply obey.

THE SERVANT GIRL AND THE BUTLER

Holar.

At first Ragna could not so much as look at the great cathedral without being consumed by the humiliation she had been made to suffer there a decade earlier. It still stung. The Holar site was expansive and incorporated many buildings, most of them tall and made of fine wood. Over everything towered St. Mary's Cathedral with its great timber walls and roof made of tin, the tall bell tower always in one's line of vision, no matter how one tried to avoid it. Looks of condemnation wherever she went. Not that anyone said anything.

Thankfully she had little time to wallow in angst. There was much to be done, as the servants had taken the utmost advantage of a prior lack of discipline. She soon came to understand that it did not serve her well to complain to the bishop about them, for he used the rod unsparingly, and this fortified any opposition against him. The seeds of that opposition had first been sown when he drove away the *officialis in spiritualibus*, the vicar Father Jon Palsson, who was renowned for his poetry written to glorify the Holy Mary. Jon was generally popular and now held a post at Grenjadarstadur in Thingeyjarsysla district.

Thus Ragna tried to tread a fine line; she rewarded those who were obedient and cut the food rations of the rebellious, told on no one and spoke ill of no one, sewed in the weaving hall with the women, and even took it upon herself to perform the household duties, time permitting. The priests and deacons were her superiors, the servants her inferiors. Here, as elsewhere, she stood alone.

Michael was contented, at least he suggested as much when she asked, and the rector, Father Kari, praised his aptitude for learning. For the first time ever they slept in separate quarters, she in a chamber separated with panels from the women's hall, he with the other schoolboys. Sometimes they did not see each other for days, save for briefly during morning mass.

Thorkell was one of the teachers, along with other, more learned priests on the site. He lectured the schoolboys on the various things he had learned during his studies abroad. Ragna found this both strange and ironic. She would never have imagined that it would come to this—that he, of all people, would end up instructing her son. It felt as if his gaze was permanently fixed on her when she served at the bishop's high table, and it made her uncomfortable. She tried looking away until she ran out of patience and gave him a sharp look back, only to become flustered once more, for he had a tendency then to send her a familiar smile, like an old friend who knew her better than she knew herself. For whatever reason, she felt his magnetic pull and was drawn to him like a moth to a flame; she felt the heat on her wings and knew that, sooner rather than later, something would happen.

No words passed between them until one day when he sent instructions for her to speak to him in the great hall where he kept the bishop's books. That same morning the servant girl Brynhildur had been brought in, who had fled from service earlier that fall to the home of her parents. The girl had refused to speak to a soul, but when Ragna confronted her in private, she revealed through gritted teeth that Thorlakur the butler had his hands on her constantly, and when she refused do his bidding, he had violated her, and she wished him dead and herself, too, if she was forced to remain at Holar. Ragna hardly knew what to say; she did not want to believe it, although she knew the butler to be capable of many transgressions. Still, she told Brynhildur that she would support her insofar as she could.

Brynhildur shook her head despondently, despite Ragna's pledge of support. "You don't know how it is. It's like you're not a person because you own nothing. Not even yourself," she said bitterly.

Although it would come to mind later, Ragna made no mention of this response when an hour later she recounted the girl's predicament to Thorkell, standing next to his writing desk in the great hall.

He surprised her with his coldness. "Brynhildur's accusations are irrelevant to this case," he said, "even though they are probably true. In any case, the charges against the butler cannot be proved. The important thing is to reiterate to the servants that desertion will not be tolerated, especially now, when there is a perpetual shortage of domestics."

"But why not ask other servants whether they will support the girl's accusations?" Ragna asked.

"It's of no use," said Thorkell. "Mr. Craxton has already decided on the fine. The girl should consider herself fortunate to be able to pay it off through work. She could just as easily have been flogged—but the bishop is too practical for that. And it is difficult for him to punish Thorlakur the butler, as he is brother to Father Jon Palsson, previously the *officialis* in matters of the church. There is enough discord over that affair as it is."

"Has he already decided on the fine?" Ragna repeated, scarcely believing what she was hearing. "How can that be? What about the panel of judges that will be called together today?"

Thorkell shrugged. "Men know what is expected of them."

Ragna was speechless. "But what if Thorlakur is guilty?" she finally asked. "Is there nothing to be done?"

"It is her word against his. Why should anyone believe a young servant girl over a grown man who has been appointed butler? Send her down around noon to be given the ruling." He waved a hand in the direction of the door to indicate that the conversation was over, and turned back to his desk.

"How small men's hearts can be," said Ragna calmly and quit the room, letting the door slam shut behind her.

That afternoon, a panel of six judges made up of canons and laymen ruled that Brynhildur's parents should pay a fine of fifteen marks for removing their daughter from service when she had been hired as a domestic for twelve months. Brynhildur herself was ordered to pay a fine of thirty marks for her desertion. The fine was to be paid in the coins of the realm by the end of the term of agreed service, otherwise the girl would have to work it off, meaning the bishop would deduct it from her wages. By Ragna's calculations, it would take Brynhildur at least another year and a half in the service of the bishop to work off the debt.

❖

It was the dairymaids who found her. She had hung herself by a leather belt that was later discovered to have been taken from the butler. She had tied it over a beam in the cowshed, climbed up on a three-footed milking stool, and kicked it away beneath her. When they had taken her down and laid her on the floor, it became clear that her belly had begun to expand. She had killed her unborn child with her.

"God damn that Thorlakur," one of the farmhands muttered. Ragna got down on one knee next to the girl and lowered her eyelids over her staring eyes. Her neck was badly bruised; it had taken a long time for her to suffocate in the noose. Ragna felt a hot tear push into the corner of her eye but steeled herself and instructed the men to carry the girl into the mortuary so she could be washed and prepared for burial. A thick smell of bodily fluids rose from the corpse and the puddle of urine that had formed on the floor beneath it. Small rivulets of liquid ran into the manure.

Thorkell arrived at that same moment, half-running; someone had reported the incident down at the school. His face drained of color when he saw the corpse, and he crossed himself.

"She cannot be buried in the churchyard, you know that," he said, his voice hollow. "She has committed murder. That is an unpardonable crime."

"You killed her," said Ragna, her voice trembling. "The butler, the bishop, the judges, and you, the priests—you tied the noose around her neck and kicked the stool from under her!"

"Hold your tongue, woman!" Thorkell replied angrily. Yet she saw that he was shocked, as was she, and that he knew she was speaking the truth. "Whatever the reasons that led to this heinous act, the girl took her own life, knowing full well that those who murder themselves are barred from resting in consecrated earth. Yet she did not let that stop her, also knowing that the bairn would be without salvation and that it would be her fault."

"A curse upon your justice!" Ragna spat out, caring nothing about the others' furtive glances.

Thorkell made no reply. "Dig her a grave to the north of the churchyard. Four yards from the wall," he ordered, speaking to the farmhands.

They stood there, frozen, and looked uncertainly at Ragna.

"Now!" Thorkell demanded. Ragna lowered her head in concession, and only then did the men obey. There was no opposing that which had prevailed since the beginning of time.

When the workers had gone off to perform their duties, the two of them remained behind with the corpse.

"I can say a prayer for her," Thorkell said quietly.

She looked at him, surprised. "You would do that? Why?"

"She was a child of God, whatever else there was," he said. "And it would ease your mind, would it not?"

"Then do it at the grave, and have her buried in the right direction."

"I cannot do that. It is forbidden."

"Then you are a coward." She said it as though she had expected nothing more from him; as if she were talking to a common laborer.

He looked as though she had slapped him. "I'll pray for her after night mass," he said after a brief silence. "If you'll keep this between you and me. If anyone finds out, I will be discharged from office."

❖

Ragna had begun to think he would not keep his word when he finally arrived at the grave, a good while past night mass. She was freezing from the wait but said nothing, not wanting to risk having him leave again. Thorkell held a Holyrood in one hand and a small lantern in the other to cast a dim light into the darkness.

She saw that he was wearing an embroidered chasuble over his black tunic; the wind took hold of the hem and blew it back and forth. The lantern shone weakly across Brynhildur's grave. There was a rough wooden cross that had been stuck into the earth that day, on the western side, by the corpse's feet. The girl lay inverse in the grave. On Judgment Day, Brynhildur Gudmundsdottir, resurrected, would have her back turned to the Savior and the dawn.

Thorkell handed Ragna the lantern and clasped the Holyrood in both of his hands, said a quiet prayer, and then raised his deep voice in song, singing in Latin. She recognized the words: he was singing a requiem for the girl, asking for peace for her soul and safekeeping by the Father, the Son, and the Holy Ghost. The cold northern wind caught the prayers and whisked them up into the starlit sky where they became a band of northern lights that wafted through the celestial heavens, first white, then green and blue, then violet; pure beauty flowing above them. Ragna felt her heart swell with humility in the face of all creation. But only for a moment. Before she knew it, the anger returned, washed over her like it had when she saw the girl hanging from the beam in the cowshed and they became one and the same woman, the past, the present, and the irreversible future. She glared at the man who stood there singing at the grave, he who had bastard children spread far and wide. Did he feel guilt, or was a requiem for a self-murderer enough to clear his conscience?

He finished, made the sign of the cross over the grave, and turned to Ragna. "Let's go. We can do no more for this wretched soul."

He took the lantern in one hand and Ragna's arm with the other, guiding her along the gravelly path by the side of the churchyard and down past the great cathedral. She felt chilled to the bone, but warmth emanated from him, like he had been standing next to a hearth.

"Brynhildur's parents should know that she received a requiem and a blessing," said Ragna when they came to the step in front of the women's hall.

"You promised to say nothing," answered Thorkell.

"I promised no such thing." She pulled her arm away. "They would not expose you, and it would give them peace."

"I sang for the soul of the dead woman, not for those of the living."

"Are they less deserving of mercy than she who fled from the battle and left them with all the distress?"

Thorkell was taken aback by her question and did not answer right away.

"Do what you feel is right," he finally said. "But do not make too much of these people's distress. Their poverty has been caused by their many children. And now they will have to pay the entire fine on their own."

❖

Despite being buried inversely and outside the churchyard, one might think that Brynhildur would rest calmly in her grave until judgment day, seeing that an ordained priest had sung over her grave. But it was quite the opposite. Within a few weeks, her ghost began to make itself known, first by rattling pots and pans in the kitchen, later by snatching food from the pantry. In the boys' quarters she walked the floors at night making the floorboards creak, particularly near the butler's bed. He still denied having got her pregnant, but to most people it was clear that first and foremost it was he who was responsible for her unrest. The bishop allowed consecrated water to be sprinkled on her grave on All Saints' Day, but it made no difference; nearly every night the butler woke up with a start and the taste of earth in his mouth. An infant could frequently be heard crying in the kitchen, even though no infant was near. Ragna paid no heed to the talk of the domestics at first, suspecting it more likely that the living were to blame for the disappearance of provisions from the pantry, and knowing that the butler's conscience tormented him at night. It did not take much to set off rumors of apparitions, and such stories might even prove beneficial for some.

Then one day, late in December, she herself became aware of strange sounds in the kitchen. She had gone there to meet with Thorlakur about preparations for the upcoming Yule feast, but she had not found him there. To her surprise, none of the domestics were there either. The kitchen was unusually empty. She was just about to leave when she heard the sound. It was soft, like the crying of a kitten. She began to look around to see if a cat was trapped somewhere, but she found nothing. Instead, the sound became more well-defined. It was the unmistakable crying of an infant, and it came from underneath her feet, up through the floorboards. Ragna crossed herself and recited the Lord's Prayer while she continued looking around, finally getting down on her knees and putting her ear to the floor. At that, the crying grew more intense. Behind her she heard someone enter; it was the butler. He was a large, portly, middle-aged man with a pallid complexion; his eyes were swollen, and there were dark circles beneath them. He had that sour, cloying smell of those who drink liquor both morning and night.

The crying grew more pained.

The butler jumped back, pale and distraught. "This must stop," he cried, "I cannot bear any more." He teetered on his feet, clasped his hands over his ears, and squeezed his eyes shut. It was of no use—the noise inside his head was maddening, and he began to whimper, begging for peace.

"Stop, stop!" he whined pathetically.

Ragna stood up and retreated toward the door. "I'll fetch Thorkell," she said breathlessly and ran out.

She nearly ran into him on the doorstep. He was standing there almost as though he had been waiting for the call, dressed in black, like a raven among the pure, white snow that blanketed everything. There were no footsteps behind him, nor anywhere else in the vicinity. Had it snowed so much since she went in?

Thorkell followed Ragna wordlessly into the kitchen, where they found Thorlakur bawling on the floor, the soft crying of the infant still coming from somewhere in the corner. Ragna hesitated in the doorway, but Thorkell gave her a small push.

"Do not be afraid," he whispered in her ear. "You have nothing to fear." Because of the way he said it, she was filled with trust, and her terror subsided.

Thorkell stuck the toe of his boot into the butler's rear. "Don't lie there, man, get up," he said harshly. "Tell me why Brynhildur and her child are haunting you. You must confess your guilt and repent if you wish to find peace!"

"I did nothing, nothing, nothing; I only did what she herself wanted," sobbed the man on the floor.

"You know she didn't want it. Don't you think she'd be lying peacefully now in her grave if she had, you wretch?"

The butler writhed, wormlike. "What shall I do? I'll do anything!"

"Confess!" The word was like the lashing of a whip.

"I confess, I confess that I forced her will and hurt her," blubbered the man on the floor. "God in heaven knows that I regret it. Just tell me, Father, what I must do to repent."

"It is not for me to order your punishment. You must make your confession to the bishop and perform the penance that he gives you."

Thorlakur stopped sniffling and looked up, alarmed. "Never. That foreign monk might just as well have me whipped at the church doors like a common criminal!"

Thorkell shrugged. "Perhaps. But you don't have many options."

Silence, save for the soft wailing from beneath the floor.

"Release me from this torment, and I will do whatever you order me to do," said the butler miserably and looked down again at the boots of the priest. Ragna said nothing, simply observed the expressions of the two men and sensed something unsaid, something that they both knew.

"Go to Grenjadarstadur and tell your brother Jon the truth. He can impose the appropriate penance. Let me have it in writing that you have left this post of your own free will, and I shall speak to Mr. Craxton on your behalf."

Thorlakur clambered to his feet. "And what about Brynhildur?"

"I will conjure her into the grave when you are gone from this place."

The butler glanced at Ragna. "What about her?"

"She is a witness to our agreement," Thorkell replied. "She will keep quiet if you keep your end of the bargain."

"But I—" Ragna began, stopping short when Thorkell looked at her sharply. He produced a scrap of vellum and handed it to the butler. A strange circular symbol was drawn on it, with hooks extending outward in all directions.

"Place this symbol on the headboard where you sleep," he said. "That will strengthen the force of the exorcism and help keep the spirit away from you."

"Yes, sir."

Butler Thorlakur Palsson left Holar without bidding farewell to a single person. He did, however, leave behind a letter for the bishop in which he explained his departure, saying that he was needed by his brother's side at Grenjadarstadur and was thus forced to give up his post at Holar without the proper termination notice. That same night, ignes fatui and flashes of lightning were seen above Brynhildur's grave to the north of the church-yard, and clumps of earth were said to have been hurled into the air, the apparition like a lightning ball that hurtled across the earth and brought ill tidings.

Someone could be seen out there, wearing a cloak, and the apparition vanished.

Ragna remained silent about all she had heard and seen. She almost told His Grace the bishop the whole story, but decided against it in the end. What business was it of hers if he decried Thorlakur for his desertion and the bad blood intensified between Grenjadarstadur and Holar? Why should she help defend such a violator? Perhaps she also felt somewhat privileged to have the confidence of Thorkell Gudbjartsson, a man who held such sway over people's souls, both here on earth and on the other side.

MY FLESH LONGS FOR YOU

Never before had so many guests been invited to the Yule celebrations at Holar. Nearly three hundred people came to spend the holidays with the bishop and the chapter. Yet that was not the only thing that was memorable about the event. There was also a general feeling of joy, of people allowing themselves to hope that the coming year would bring good fortune. The winter had been surprisingly mild, just like the last one. Many had prospered from the Great Plague—one man's misery is another man's fortune—and in many a weary heart stirred the hope that toil and hardship were behind them for the time being, that surely the Almighty could see that this tiny nation in the northern seas had atoned enough.

The violent acts of English ship crews during the recent fishing season could hardly be taken into account, and anyway, those were the deeds of men, and had nothing to do with divine powers. Tales of stolen fish and the kidnapping of children were exchanged at the Yule feast, and there was as much discontent over these tidings as ever. Some, including Thorsteinn from Akrar, maintained that the children had not been taken by force, but rather that the poor had simply handed them over in return for flour and other commodities. They had done this to save the rest of their brood from starvation. Some had even willingly joined the English. Be that as it may, most agreed that

Bishop Craxton was better than none, even if he was English, and that he would soon have his countrymen under control; after all, he seemed clever, and surely the English ribalds would obey someone who was said to be on friendly terms with King Henry himself.

The bishop provided food and drink in abundance, and he was amiable and courteous to his guests. However, Father Jon Palsson at Grenjadarstadur and all of his followers were conspicuously absent. In the darkened corners of the room, the guests discussed the likely consequences of such a purposeful omission, which they believed could be dire.

In this manner, news was related and discussed, but Ragna had limited time for such concerns. With the butler gone and no replacement as yet, her responsibilities had increased manifold. It was up to her to make sure that there was plenty to eat and drink, that guests were seated at tables according to rank so that no one was offended, and that the food was presented in a way that befitted a bishopric. Still, Ragna thought the gusto with which some of the good farmers imbibed the English ale quite appalling. Her parents both held seats of honor, with Thorsteinn at the bishop's high table, next to Ormur Loftsson, the king's governor. Opposite him sat Thorkell. With some apprehension she observed their exchange, as far as she was able; it seemed to her that they were getting along fairly well. The lawman was in good spirits and seemed in no mood to revive bygones. When she brought wine for the bishop and his companions, her foster-father gave her a broad smile. She put two large, heavy jugs on the table and meant to withdraw, but he placed a hand on her arm.

"Men speak highly of you, Ragna," he said. "Father Thorkell says that the management of Holar is better than ever, now that you have been given the keys to the pantry and parlor."

She glanced at Thorkell and almost expected to see a hint of mockery in his eyes. Instead, they were tender. She was embarrassed, and felt her cheeks turn crimson.

"She is modest, too, and well-behaved," said Thorsteinn, evidently pleased, and released his hold on her arm. "That is just how women should be. If only more were like this, all would be well. Then there would be no need for men to invoke the law to keep their wives, like that old beggar Skeggi Alason in Slettuhlid."

The men around the table laughed. The matter of Skeggi and his wife Thordis was well known: she ran away on a regular basis, each time claiming that she had been forced into the conjugal bed against her will, although a full ten winters had passed since she had been given to her husband in the presence of witnesses. Thorkell smiled and leaned forward, shaking his head.

"Ah, but there we disagree, good lawman. Women who have no passion are a poor catch, and Ragna's temper is surely equal to that of stalwarts like Thordis Magnusdottir, when the occasion warrants. Also, let us not forget who joined Thordis and Skeggi in matrimony and subsequently dismissed her claims, while accepting a handsome payment in return. It was the man who now sits in the best parish in North Iceland at the invitation of the archbishop in Nidaros, in blatant opposition to the rightful ecclesiastical authorities here at Holar."

The men grew quiet, and some sent Thorkell a cold glance, while others grinned to themselves. All of them were well aware of the recent power struggles at Holar. Opinions were divided as to who was more fit for leadership among the priests, Father Jon Palsson, with his many years of experience as a priest and vicar of Holar see, or the ambitious Thorkell Gudbjartsson, who had been educated abroad and was endowed with a keen intellect, although he was still young, and moreover favored trade with the English. It was clear to everyone that the latter had the upper hand, for the time being at least, since Jon Palsson was a sworn adversary of the English and loyal to his hereditary king. He had, on top of everything, managed to capture the parish of Grenjadarstadur with the aid of the archbishop in Norway while Holar was without a bishop. Yet bishops came and went, and even the mighty could fall, as history had proven, time and again.

Thorsteinn Olafsson got to his feet. "I say we drink to all women, those with a temper as well as the well behaved," he said, lifting his goblet high into the air. "Yet those who have chosen the church as their bride should be the last to advise the rest of us how to handle our wives. Still, they are forgiven, for they know not what they do, as the Good Book says!" Laughter rang out, and trouble was averted, although Thorsteinn's barbed words did not go unnoticed among those familiar with earlier events.

Ragna took the empty wine jugs from the table and hastened from the room.

◈

The loud voices and laughter stopped, people shushed their dogs who quarreled over bones on the floor, and even those who were already drunk grew quiet when the quivering tones of the harp sounded through the hall: bright, true, sacred, driving out all evil.

In a deep voice, the harpist began to sing a hymn from the Psalter of King David:

"*O God, you are my God, early will I seek you; my soul thirsts for you.*"

The sounds of the instrument were strong and cleansing; strange that such beautiful tones might be conjured from mere animal intestines, stringed between pegs across a wooden panel.

"My flesh longs for you."

Ragna listened to Thorkell, enraptured. Was there not something unholy about the passion in his voice, or for a song of worship to be infused with this sort of mournful longing—even lust? She tried to look away but could not; she found herself falling, becoming lost in the deep blue of his eyes.

"My mouth shall praise you with joyful lips, when I remember you upon my bed, and meditate on you in the night watches..."

Later that evening, musicians from among John Craxton's entourage performed. They had accompanied him from abroad and were said to have performed at court back in England. They blew into bulky krummhorns, conjuring dark and gloomy tones, and sang a song of worship. When they had finished, they put the horns away and took out pipes and tambourines. Vibrant tones filled the darkened hall with playfulness and joy, and the tambourine beat a quick rhythm. The guests looked at the bishop, and each other, with surprise. Those who had been abroad had heard frolicsome music performed by charlatans and fools. Was this not inappropriate at a bishopric, to say nothing of at a Yule feast? What sort of capricious individual was this foreigner, anyway, who had come to settle at Holar in Hjaltadalur Valley?

The bishop smiled. "The psalms of David tell us to praise the Lord with the timbrel and dance, with stringed instruments and organs," he said. "Good neighbors, let us obey the Word of God and celebrate, for a Savior is born!"

Before too long the boldest among the guests were on the floor, hesitant at first, allowing themselves to be carried by the music. Hearts beat faster and feet took unfamiliar steps, almost of their own accord, and hands touched in tandem with the feverish beat of the tambourine.

Ragna watched from a distance, feeling the tones swirl all around her, seductive and inviting, yet she remained stoic in the face of temptation. Then she felt someone catch her hand, and in an instant she was in the midst of a circular dance and Thorkell was holding on to her shoulders, laughing and happy, an entirely different man from the one he had been a moment before the harp playing began. She could not help smiling too, and she had to work to keep up with him.

Then he was gone, and the bishop himself stood in front of her. He bowed deeply, took her hand, and pulled her to him in a strange, foreign dance. To her great dismay, Ragna felt all eyes upon them.

"Allow me to lead. Hold up the hem of your skirt so that you don't trip, and you'll be fine," said Craxton smiling, his gray eyes gleaming with excitement. She obeyed, and before she knew it, they were alone in the middle of the floor in front of the musicians and the bishop was performing complex steps with his hands on his hips, indicating that she should do the same. She tried to keep her dignity and mimic his dexterity, but her face was flushed and her chest heavy. One of the onlookers suppressed a laugh. It was as if the teasing trills of the flute underscored her lack of skill, and she looked helplessly at the bishop, silently begging for help. To her great relief, he took her hand and bowed to indicate that the dance was over, and the people applauded their bishop and his housekeeper. Ragna hurried out of the room, desperate to leave the throng and breathe in some fresh air.

He was waiting for her in the dimly lit hallway, pulled her into a dark alcove and whispered bitterly: "Did you like dancing with

John Craxton and having all those men ogle you and lust after you?!" She was stunned and could not utter a sound. Thorkell continued, rapidly, forcefully: "It pained me more than it ever has to see you smile at him, to see you smile at any other man. Know that you are meant for me, that you have been mine from the beginning."

Did she have a choice? At that very instant, she might have seen a twinkle of derangement in his gaze; she might have shoved him aside, along with everything implied by his words. Rejected him as he had rejected her, as he had degraded and humiliated her. But perhaps it was too late; perhaps she had no other choice but to love him, to desire to please him, to make him happy. What did she have to lose? Why not accept the love he offered her, hoping that somehow everything would work out in the future as it had in the past? Only the heart knows its own agony, and no one can interfere, even in its joy.

"Dearest," she said. "I am yours. Forgive me."

His eyes reflected back her own beauty, her strength and abilities, and her faith in all possibility. There was no turning back.

He led her into a small room behind the great hall, where the bishop's rulings and decrees were recorded in books, and where his letters and indictments were kept. It smelled of ink and manuscript scrolls and power. Through the thick, paneled turf walls they could hear the merriment of the feast.

Thorkell turned the key in the lock, took the thick woolen cape from his shoulders, and laid it out on the floor.

Nothing mattered but this, to open buckles and ribbons, buttons and belts, find and touch naked skin, stroke and caress, kiss and lick, bite, grasp, open, give and receive, hold tight and hard, become one in the surge, two bodies wet with perspiration, loud noises as their hips came together. He moaned as he increased and decreased the speed of his thrusts, whereas she was more quiet, meek against his intensity and lack of restraint.

When he reached his climax, he pulled away and spilled his seed on her. Hot, white rivulets on a hot, white belly. Salty-sweet scent.

Beloved; beloved. Afterward she rose up on one elbow and gazed into his face, scrutinized him with an insatiable look, wondered at his muscular body and the way the lines next to his mouth and eyes were gone now. He was like a small boy. Beloved; beloved. The slight hint of a smile at the sides of his mouth, as though he was self-conscious in their intimacy, though she could not be sure since he had shut his eyes to protect himself from her intrusion into his thoughts. She could see his eyes moving beneath the lids, but she said nothing and asked nothing. She wanted to know what would happen next, yet at the same time she did not want to know; longed for it, yet at the same time feared it above all else.

Fatigue washed over her, and she lay down next to Thorkell, nestled into the crook of his arm, wishing for security in a world that seemed more uncertain than ever before. No sooner have we been given something before we begin to fear the gift, fear that we are undeserving and that it will be snatched away in an instant. And so she stroked him, moved her fingers slowly across his broad shoulders and arms, down his chest with its bristly hairs, to his belly, down along his thighs and in between them, cupped him in her fingers, feeling him, owning the memory of him, whatever would later come to pass.

Thorkell's chest rose and fell, his breath slow and deep, as if he were asleep, although she suspected that he was awake.

❧

How have I been able to live and breathe without knowing this man, without knowing the passion of loving? His every glance gives my life meaning, his every smile, every touch. His existence is the reason I wake up each morning. Our opportunities to meet in private are few and hence all the more precious; his intensity is invaluable proof that I am finally worth something, that he needs me as much as I need him. No one has ever known me as well as he does. I too know the depth and breadth of his soul, and we are one. Very occasionally the thought creeps in that perhaps we do not know each other at all, but I refuse to allow such doubts to upset me. Now is all there is and all that matters.

❧

One day, near the Feast of St. Paul, Ragna came upon Thorkell in the library. He was writing on a manuscript scroll all manner of strange symbols and scribbles in red ink, secret runes of some kind, from ancient times. She was deeply shaken and could not conceal it.

He laughed at her anxious expression and stroked the underside of her chin with the quill, a black raven's feather, moving it down into the shadow between her breasts, then up again, tickling her nose. "It is not as if the ink is made from the blood of virgins, my lovely," he said kindly. "No need for such a terrified expression."

She stammered something incoherent in response, and he became annoyed. He picked up sheets of vellum covered in writing from the desk and thrust them in front of her.

"Look here, little fool. It is only a text about the variable illnesses and natural responses of the body, prayers to halt bleeding and separate infants from their mothers, charms, wrestling magic, and suchlike that may prove useful and bring harm to no one."

"Wrestling magic…" she said, and her voice trembled. "A relatively harmless *galdur* perhaps, but a *galdur* nevertheless. And what are you writing with those magic runes, designed to deceive? Thorkell, why do you do this?"

He took hold of her shoulders.

"My sweet Ragna, you who are closest and dearest to my heart, surely you can see that I must practice all that I have studied so that I will not forget it. I must learn as much as I can, for that is the only true power that a man has, over himself if nothing else—though gaining power over others is also useful. This can be possible only through the art of learning, and the knowledge that is hidden from others." He grew agitated and went on excitedly: "Nothing is more important in this mortal life than understanding the machinations of this world and the world beyond, the world that is invisible to mortals, and to gain an understanding of the forces that govern them—both good and evil."

He let go of her, turned, and stuffed the manuscript into a gray sealskin folder that he tied with a narrow string.

"I must use the secret runes in my Graskinna manuscript to keep this exclusive knowledge—useful to only a few—from falling into the hands of corrupt men. That is the only reason, dear Ragna. Everything I have gathered and written pertaining to the medical arts, bloodletting, healing, herbal balms and broths is written in a script that is easy to read. Some of it is even written in Nordic."

She did not dare to argue further, but fear had settled in her heart and would not be repealed. What if the bishop learned of this sorcery? Surely it was only a matter of time, since Michael had told her that the schoolboys chattered about it amongst themselves, and on more than one occasion, she had had to bite her tongue when he brought her the strange tales of Thorkell that were being related among them.

She kept her double life carefully concealed from Michael, though sometimes she wondered whether he sensed that something was different from before. In a way she was surprised that he had not confronted her with it, considering how close they had always been and how jealous he became if he felt she was favoring others over him. But everything was different now. Michael was changed, too, she felt that, and she was seized by loneliness when she saw how quickly the time passed and how soon he would be fully grown and gone from her. Her longing to have Thorkell near her grew even stronger at these thoughts, and when she felt the intensity of her love for him, it made her almost desperate. What if he betrayed her trust again?

They met only in secret, and Thorkell seemed to enjoy taking the risk. Many times he claimed to have business in the kitchen, and when the domestics looked the other way, he would plant a kiss on Ragna's neck or inconspicuously slip her something small, like a bit of burnt sugar. She was on edge until he left again, and she scolded him harshly for his conduct when they were alone. He only laughed and caressed her as no one had ever done, tickled the soles of her feet with his toes so that she giggled, and she could not help feeling proud that he was willing to take such risks, just to demonstrate his love for her.

For it was risky indeed. His position was at stake, and thereby all his future hopes. Even though throughout the centuries priests in Iceland had been known to keep mistresses and to adopt the children that they had fathered, one by one, surely Craxton, who had taken his vows in the Franciscan order, would not tolerate any priest close to him breaking the vow of celibacy.

How greatly her life had changed within a short space of time, and how little it would take for everything to collapse into the sand on which it was built. But she avoided such thoughts and instead looked out at the world with new eyes, seeing beauty wherever she looked: the winter firn on the home field glittering in the fickle sunshine at noon, the stars in heaven brighter than they were before, the silver crescent moon in the black winter sky clearer and more distinct than ever.

❖

His intensity frightened her. It also enraptured her.

"Promise that you will never betray me, Ragna," said Thorkell one night at the beginning of the month of Goa, in early spring, when they met in the small back room. For a full week they had not been alone together, as he had been away on business with John Craxton. Before she knew it, he had brandished a knife and cut his palm, his bloodied hand reaching out for hers. Hesitantly she extended her right hand, and he used the knife again. Her blood swelled from the wound, and she merged her blood with his, promising him loyalty unto death in this ancient manner. A few drops fell on the floor between them.

"Now you are mine in the pagan manner," he said and smiled, the priest, with fire in his eyes that made her burn, inside and out.

They consummated their oath up against the wall, with blood running both from Ragna's palm and from between her legs. In the dark he did not notice, and afterward he was clearly upset, even shaken. But how could that be? He who feared nothing, not even her. She had not told him that she was bleeding, and she now registered the smell, thick and slightly sour, and apologized.

"You are unclean," he said sharply. "You should have told me."

"I...I'm sorry," she stammered, ashamed, and felt to her greater dismay how her eyes stung from the harsh tone of his voice. "But..."

"But what?"

"What we are doing is acceptable to neither God nor men anyway," she said, speaking rapidly, astonished at her own boldness. "Why should we keep to convention in these matters and not in others?"

"Menstrual blood is unclean," he replied. "It is the blood of death, not of life, and it saps a man's energy. And precisely now I need all my energy, as never before."

A tear rolled down her cheek. His anger dissipated somewhat when he saw he had made her cry.

"But how could you know that, my dearest, you who are so innocent and so good." He wiped her tear away with his index finger. "Don't cry. I forgive you. Your ignorance is not your fault." He kissed her cheek, and all was well between them once again.

She did not ask why he needed to be more energetic than other men precisely now, though she suspected the reason. It was being whispered that, at Thorkell's instigation, the bishop planned to relieve Grenjadarstadur Parish of the noncompliant Father Jon Palsson. No parish in North Iceland had farms that were more prosperous, and Craxton would certainly have been able to make good use of the tax money that the clerk was surreptitiously said to have sent to the archbishop in Nidaros, rather than using it to maintain the church at Grenjadarstadur as he should have done. No doubt His Grace the bishop would appoint a loyal servant of Holar cathedral to oversee this prosperous parish, and he would reward him handsomely. Ragna made no comment when this came up among the domestics. Schemes relating to temporal affluence and power were none of her concern, nor theirs, she felt.

FROM THE RIB OF A MAN

The sun rose higher in the sky, the days grew longer, and the first grass began to sprout alongside the retreating snow banks. Winter was over, and at long last the northern hemisphere welcomed the arrival of spring. Frost evaporated from the ground and the Hjaltadalur River rid itself of ice, so the mid-winter gloom and smell of staid urine could finally be washed from the linens. Ragna ordered that the bedding be removed from all the beds, sheets as well as blankets, and the girls knelt on the riverbank for days on end, washing and scrubbing, rinsing and wringing. Even with hands that were blue from the cold, they had perpetual smiles on their faces, for the sun was brilliant in a clear blue sky and the earthy smell of the newly thawed marsh filled their senses.

Ragna monitored the girls closely, letting them know if something needed improvement and if they had done enough, even helping them lay the bedding out on the gnarled birch trees to dry, though strictly speaking it was not her duty. The smell of clean linen lifted her spirits, and she felt a childlike glee when the southern breeze blew the sheets to and fro on the branches.

With one hand she gathered and lifted her long skirts, and headed into the spinney, pushing through the thick branches that were already sprouting buds, inhaling the scent of fresh vegetation and moist earth. She sank into the soft ground in some places, her boots leaving deep imprints. The wagtails, newly arrived from their winter sojourn in milder climes, tweeted cheerfully in the shrubs, and from the marsh not far off came the trilling of a whimbrel. The white, fuzzy buds on the broad-leaved willows were already swollen, on the verge of blossoming and scattering their seeds.

When Ragna headed back to the river a while later, she could hear Thorkell's deep, resounding voice. She smiled to herself at the warm feeling that welled up in her and how her heart beat faster just from the sound of it. He was talking to Gudrun, one of the servant girls, and did not see her.

"Don't worry, we'll find a way," he said, his hand on Gudrun's belly. "When is it due?" Gudrun looked up and saw Ragna standing there, motionless, paralyzed.

The girl placed her hand on top of Thorkell's. "In the fall, dear friend. I know I can rely on you in this matter as in all the others, always."

Ragna turned and began walking quickly, without uttering a word. She did not know if Thorkell had seen her. She did not look back, just made haste along the riverbank. When she reached a small hill and was out of sight, she began to run. Her feet got tangled in her skirts and she tripped on a tussock, falling forward onto the withered grass. She lay on her belly, breathing heavily, not crying, digging her spread fingers into the ground, searching for something to hold on to. Maybe she had really seen nothing, heard nothing; indeed, she was not even sure anything had happened, but even so, she knew that the most hurtful thing of all had already taken place. Burning hot tears forced their way into her eyes, but she squeezed them shut, blocking the exits, in a desperate attempt to deny that which already was. Instead, they collected and turned into a hard lump of ice in her chest, and the blood that had burned for him slowly turned cold in her veins. She could feel her heartbeat and her breathing become steadier, and she grew calmer, sensing her aloneness like never before, yet also her strength. When she opened her eyes, they were dry.

A long-legged spider clambered through the grass next to her face. Ragna saw its dew-covered silver web through the dry straws, so efficiently spun, speckled with flies. She moved her hand and let the spider crawl into her palm, closed her hand around it, felt it tickle as it searched frantically for a way out of the dark.

"Begone then, leggy beast," she whispered, opened her palm, and blew the spider swiftly into the air and to its freedom. It rushed off on its agile legs, leaving its silver web behind.

After a long while, Ragna rose to her feet, dusted herself off, and walked slowly back to the houses.

❖

How can I both love him and hate him? How is it that I cannot stand having him near me, yet cannot bear the thought of losing him? Does he not love his offspring above all else, as I do, and then also the woman who gives birth to his flesh and blood? Almighty Lord, have mercy on me, take away this agony, this ice-cold burning in my chest.

Each time we have made love I have risked my life. Even afterward, as I pour the herbal potion that he brewed for me into a spoon, I cannot be sure that a new life will not awaken in my belly. If it does, I will surely die. And yet I grieve each time I start to bleed, and the white-hot jealousy will not leave me, for I know I shall never be equal to his other women in this way. Our flesh and blood will never be one. Never—such a terrible word, so final.

Why, why is everything this way? I want to rail at him, to wound him as I have been wounded. But I am a coward. I cannot bear his disapproval on top of everything else. How spineless I am. But what can I do? I love him, even more than before, even knowing how untrustworthy he is. Is it perhaps because I know and sense how tenuous his love is for me? What other choice do I have but to stop loving him, and how will I live if I do? Yes, the price is agonizing pain, but it is better than shivering emptiness. And no, I shall never be able to trust him again, but how can I turn him away forever? How to manage these complexities of my heart, I who am only a woman, created from the rib of a man?

❖

At first she tried to pretend that all was the same as before. The hectic spring chores helped keep her mind off other things; there was so much to do with the sun finally shining and Easter not far away. The domestics were out working in the fields each day, women as well as men. It was time-consuming work, arduous and mucky, trampling manure into the tussocked ground, and those who were put to work indoors counted their blessings. Nonetheless, many of them grumbled about the harshness of the housekeeper's demands after Lent had begun and they were allowed only bread and fish as nourishment, and only water to drink—at the bishopric, of all places. Ragna ordered them to air out all the parlors and chambers, to sweep and scrub every corner, clean out the floor rushes and dirt, and scatter fresh rushes on all the floors; everything was to be spick-and-span by the time Easter, the great feast of cleansing, arrived.

She got up for work early each morning with the servant women, was not idle for a single moment all day, and fell exhausted into bed each evening. And yet, sleep never came until the early hours, and when it did it brought nightmares, so that she woke up gasping, soaked in sweat, more tired than before she lay down to sleep. Her dreams were all very similar, at least what she remembered of them: Gudrun and Thorkell lying in each other's arms, a hoard of children in their bed, arms and legs and torsos together in one writhing pile, she herself a silent onlooker, lying on the floor in front of them, until Gudrun got out of bed and gave her a small kick, with a tinkling laugh.

Sending Gudrun out to work in the fields gave her some respite; at least then she did not have to see her in the daytime, too. Yet this was short-lived. A few days later, Thorkell appeared and told her gruffly that the girl was not fit for outdoor work on account of her perpetual nausea and vomiting. Evidently she was with child.

"Oh, is that so?" Ragna said, her eyes fixed on his face. He had not made an appearance in the kitchen for a while, though she knew he had been busy, like her. Thorkell shifted his gaze and his weight, impatiently.

"This means she does not have to observe Lent, just like the young children—as you know," he added quickly. "Go easy on her. She is in a bad state, poor wretch, and has nowhere else to go in her condition."

"Oh?" she said, her voice flat. She waited a few moments and then asked, her voice little more than a whisper: "And who is the father of the child?"

But he had turned and was gone. Perhaps he had not heard her. Probably it was for the best—she did not want to hear his answer, to hear the truth from his lips—at least not yet. It was painful enough as it was.

❖

Gudrun held her young daughter by the hand when she came to see the housekeeper on the day that farmhands were permitted to leave or enter employment, shortly before Cross Mass. She was there to offer her services to the Holar bishopric for the coming year. She was beginning to show and did not try to conceal it. She held her head high and carried herself without shame.

Ragna shook her head.

"You will have to leave," she said tersely.

"Leave?" Gudrun repeated, astonished. "Has Father Thorkell not spoken to you about my condition?"

"He has," Ragna said, cloaking her own pain to stop the tears that forced their way to her eyes and made her hands tremble. "He and I are of the same mind: that the Holar bishopric cannot support the birth of countless numbers of illegitimate children by letting such actions by the domestics go unreprimanded."

Gudrun's small daughter stared at Ragna solemnly and silently with her large, dusky blue eyes. Those eyes, everywhere she looked—a constant reminder.

"I'll not be able to get a good position anywhere else in my condition," said Gudrun, her lower lip trembling slightly. "I will have to send my Hrefna away to strangers." She pulled her daughter close and put an arm around her shoulder, as if doing so would help ward off the inevitable.

"Perhaps you should have thought of that before you..." Ragna broke off, the unspoken words hanging in the air, scornful, cruel. "You'll find work somewhere," she added. "There's a shortage of domestics, and you are a hard worker."

"I wish to plead my case to the steward. I cannot believe that he wants me to be sent away."

"He is not here."

"Where is he?"

"On an errand in South Iceland for His Grace the bishop. He left this morning and is not expected back until two or perhaps three weeks hence." Ragna had difficulty concealing the satisfaction in her voice.

"I have been in service here for two years. Before that I was at Muli in Adaldalur for several years."

Ragna made no reply.

"And you, of all women—you who should be able to understand…"

The words died in the silence, that disconcerting silence that grows louder the longer it prevails.

"Make sure you are gone before the end of the week."

◈

She had not expected him to be so angry. Had thought that his guilt would stop him from coming to her about the girl's departure.

"How could you be so heartless as to drive Gudrun away?" Thorkell's voice was the same pitch as usual, but his evident disgust for what she had done made it sound cold and harsh.

"She will not get much work done with one child under her belt and another holding onto her apron strings," answered Ragna coolly. "In fact, I find it strange that she was permitted to have the girl here, under the bishop's care, for this long. We should not be encouraging the immoral conduct of the servants by looking the other way."

"You were shown mercy, but you show no mercy to others. Is it just punishment for a woman who gives birth to a child out of wedlock to be sent begging?"

Ragna took his meaning but pretended not to, and she felt the lump of ice in her chest grow larger. How dare he compare the two of them!

"Why should she not suffer the consequences of her actions like other women?" she remarked obstinately, not realizing until too late that she had compared herself with Gudrun with her own words.

"Gudrun was kind to me, and compliant," said Thorkell. "Even though there is nothing between us now, I care for her and little Hrefna, whom she gave birth to before I went abroad to study. I promised her a long time ago that she could rely on me, and I will keep my word, even though I am flawed and have violated the law of God and of man in more ways than one. It is not for you to judge me, or her, or any other person. It is for God to judge, and for us to show compassion."

"I don't need to have your mistresses and their bastard children constantly in front of me!" Ragna heard her voice grow shrill and felt even angrier; after all, righteousness was hers, not his. She had never expected him to admit to fathering the child so readily; deep down she had hoped he would deny it and perhaps even try to convince her that the child was another man's and he had only wanted to help a poor servant girl. "When...did it happen?"

He shrugged. "She says she will give birth in the fall, so it must have been at Yuletide, perhaps the New Year. What does it matter, when you know she means nothing to me anymore?"

"At Yuletide or the New Year..." Ragna gasped for breath and brought her hands to her throat, feeling like the burning jealousy would strangle her.

Tears began to cascade from her eyes, crushed slivers of ice.

Thorkell's manner grew milder; he put his arms around her and kissed the whiteness of her neck, just below the ear where the skin is softest, letting her cry in his arms. He hummed to her as softly as a child and stroked her back with his large hand and long fingers.

"Of course it was before Yuletide, before I entertained any hope that you would submit to me…"

Ragna tried to suppress her sobs, feeling all the more humiliated when she realized that she could not cry anywhere else, no one but him could comfort her, and she grieved for it all: her shattered illusion of him and herself and the beauty of all creation. And she hated him for witnessing her agony and herself even more for loving him as much as before and for allowing herself to be soothed in his arms—by him, whom she despised in her heart for being who he was.

Ugliness settled all around her, obscuring her vision.

◈

A few days later, Thorkell left Holar early in the morning with two spare horses. He returned three days later with Gudrun and her daughter. He had found them at his father's farm, Muli in Adaldalur, where she said the father of her child, a farmhand, lived. Allegedly, she had found him on his deathbed, nearly gone from an unknown illness. By the grace of God, Thorkell had rescued her from catching whatever it was that ailed the man. She showed anyone who was interested a scroll on which the farmhand confirmed, with an almost undecipherable signature, that he was the father of both Gudrun's daughter and the unborn child. Witnesses were Father Thorkell and his father Gudbjartur.

Most people were quick to work out the truth, for there was no question that little Hrefna bore a striking resemblance to the steward at Holar, particularly the strong expression around the eyes. This was now more apparent than ever before. Besides, no one could recall Gudrun having visited Thingeyjarsysla district since she had come into service at Holar, nor the farmhand coming to visit her. The servants whispered amongst themselves, and each had their own view on the matter; some felt that Father Thorkell should be respected for doing right by the mother of his child, while others considered it disgraceful that he had broken his vow of chastity and was attempting in this way to conceal what was obvious to everyone. Moreover, he had blatantly opposed the will of Ragna, the housekeeper. Perhaps there were some scallywags who enjoyed seeing her brought down to size, the daughter of the lawman, who had given birth to a bastard herself. Those who consider themselves above the rest naturally deserve to be scorned. All are equal in the eyes of God and the classless.

❖

He says he does not care for Gudrun anymore. How can I believe him when he has gone and fetched her from another district? Was that to show me who is in charge? The servants mutter and whisper in the corners; they probably think that I have been degraded by allowing the steward to take control. A curse on those gossipmongers, may they rot in hell! They know nothing of the real reasons— except perhaps Gudrun. She may have her suspicions, as women always do with men they have known. Known...at least she has never known his heart, of that I am sure. But he will want her to believe that she has, to keep her silent about her suspicions. Yes, that must be it. He does not want our affair to become public; he wants to protect our love.

One moment I believe the things I tell myself and then all is well; the next moment I am sinking, I want to die, and I am frightened, for I have never before wanted as desperately to fall into the darkness. I fear that I may even have the courage to do what Brynhildur did, and that is a dreadful thought.

But who am I to demand his faithfulness when it was I who betrayed him in the beginning? He who moreover has broken his vows to the Holy Church for my sake, and thereby risked his soul's salvation. "Judge not, lest ye be judged," is written in the Holy Scripture.

He looks at me inquisitively, unhappily. I avoid meeting him alone. I do not want to know what awaits me in the depths of his eyes. I no longer ask him what he intends to do, for I do not even know what I want to do. What will be, must be, in the future as in the past. The birth of the child will show whether he went to her still warm from my bed—or whether it was the other way around. Does it matter, in the end, whether or not he lied? If he lied, it was for my sake, to abate my suffering. My life is all one lie. Do I know anymore what is right and what is wrong?

Why am I ashamed of myself and my stubborn feelings of love? Mary, holy mother of God, have mercy on my sinful soul!

YOUR ADVERSARY, THE DEVIL

Michael half-ran up the precipitously steep bell tower stairs, casting furtive glances over his shoulder. He stopped, listened, and then continued, taking care to tread only on the outer edges of the steps where they were least likely to creak, and skipping those that he knew made noise. To his satisfaction he heard old Hrafn the warden down below, shooing his pursuers out of the church. He was scolding them for running in the House of God and reproaching them for their immaturity and idiocy, on this of all days, when the synod was about to begin and he had plenty of other, more pressing, things to do than chasing schoolboys who should be old enough to know better.

On reaching the belfry, Michael threw himself on the floor to catch his breath, a little abashed at having fled the scene, yet also victorious. There was no way he could have tackled his tormentors, three of them together and older and bigger than he was, yet he had nonetheless managed to outrun them and was safe. Once again he had sought refuge in St. Mary's Cathedral under the protective wing of the white-haired ringer Hrafn. He rose to his knees and crawled out to the open west window, the shutters already pulled aside, knowing the bells would soon ring for mass. He cast a glance over the tents on the nearby fields, camps erected for the synod. He looked down and saw his schoolmates in front of the church door, animatedly talking amongst themselves. There was no wind, and he could hear that they were talking about him, were vowing to beat him to a pulp the next time they got hold of him, calling him a bloody Skraeling and godforsaken half-Englishman as was their wont, it not being clear which derogatory term disgusted them more.

Indignantly Michael stuck his hand in his pocket and took out a rock, raising it for the throw, but he changed his mind in time and put it back. Even if he could easily hit one of the boys from this distance, his hiding place was too valuable to sacrifice for the momentary satisfaction of revenge.

He rummaged through a pile of straw under the east wall and soon found a scrap of dried halibut. He made a face when he saw that the mice had already partaken of the goods and little more than the chewed skin of the halibut remained. Michael cursed his own foolishness, to think he could store even a scrap of food up here, where both feathered and four-legged thieves roamed, snatching and shitting as they pleased. He tossed the halibut skin to one side, annoyed.

Anyway, he wasn't particularly hungry, since it was not long past breakfast. There had been a disagreement among the boys at the table for no particular reason, as usual. One wanted more than the allocated ration and took Michael's bread, saying that since he was younger, he needed less than the rest of them. This was followed with demeaning words about his Skraeling looks. As always, they talked about him in the third person, like he wasn't there.

This was how it had been nearly his entire time at Holar. They rarely hurt him physically; instead, they excluded him from their conversations and games, never addressed him directly, talked about him but not to him, and seemed to enjoy winding him up until he lost control and hurled himself with punches and kicks at the boy closest to him. Much of the humiliation was made up of the fact that they rarely fought back. Usually there were a few of them who simply picked him up and put him outside, set him down in the muck near the front door, and closed it. If one of the priests arrived while this was going on, the boys stayed mum in unison, sticking together. He was the only one excluded and had his own side of the story, but no one paid him any attention since he was in almost perpetual conflict with the others and was already known for his quick temper.

One time he had stared long and hard into the blue-black water of the well, examining his own face reflected in the still surface, struggling to make out the features that they said were like the Skraelings in Greenland. He didn't really know what he should be looking for, except that he and his mother both had high cheekbones and a fairly wide brow and forehead. But others had that too. Finally he gave up trying to reason away their cruelty, having long since realized that it did not matter the slightest bit what was right and wrong, they would only find something else to tease him about. Their harsh words stung, even though he told himself that those morons were as worthless as the dirt under his shoes.

Stronger than most things, this need to belong, to be part of something—to be one of the group. At the very least to have your own relatives stand by you, to not be a perpetual outsider, different from the rest; a bastard.

But even though he hated the boys, he kept quiet about it to his mother. She had her own problems, and besides, he had a secret to think about and plan for. And in any case, it was not all bad at the school—sometimes it was even enjoyable. Astronomy and the movement of the planets were his passion, as were all those other things the priests shared with their pupils about the countries across the sea and all the strange and wonderful things that happened there. Sometimes they heard news about the endless war between the English and the French, and some talked about the great war tools that were used there, called catapults, used during sieges to send torrents of spears and arrows and sometimes even fireballs over castle walls. There were even stranger weapons made of crushed sulphur that made a huge explosion when lit with fire. But of course most of the time went for studying Latin. Michael sighed. Surely it would make more sense to teach the boys English so they could speak with traders and merchant sailors, and—not least—so that he would be able to speak to his father when they finally met. Mind you, he already knew the odd word in English, had learned bits and pieces from the crew of the *Christopher,* Thorsteinn's ship, and still more at Holar, where there were a number of Englishmen who were part of the bishop's entourage, and where there were frequently English visitors.

A rustling out by the wall, near the small bells. A plump mouse stuck its quivering nose into the fish skin he'd tossed aside. Probably it was so well-fed from eating all that dried fish, the little rascal. He sat perfectly still with legs outstretched, watching it. Then he heard someone taking slow, heavy steps up the stairs. The mouse rushed for cover, and the boy stood up calmly. Hrafn, the ringer, stuck his head up past the edge and gave him a nod.

"Ah, so you're still here, boy…all right, well, let's ring the bells together." And they sounded the bells like sometimes before, the boy ringing the smaller bells according to the old man's instructions, and Hrafn the larger ones. The pendulums rang out against the tin and copper, creating a divine composition, old yet new, played daily, yet never exactly the same. The clanging of the bells was so fantastically loud that the old man's hearing was nearly gone. The boy stuck little bits of wool into his ears to keep his eardrums from bursting.

Reminding Michael to get out before mass began, the ringer patted the boy's cheek, still scratched and bloody from the fight, and told him to be more careful next time. He then descended the stairs once more.

Michael promised he would take more care and remained in the belfry, looking out to see if he could see his foes. A short a distance away he saw them, under a basalt wall, looking at the procession of priests who now approached the church from the camps. Never had he seen so many clerics gathered together in one place. He hadn't even realized there were so many in the entire country. He tried to count them but found he couldn't be bothered, made a guess that there were dozens, maybe even a hundred. Most were beautifully clothed in colorfully woven chasubles; some were not quite so ostentatious, dressed in unassuming dark woolen cloaks, abbots and priors from the monasteries at Munkathvera, Thingeyrar, and Modruvellir. Some were barefoot and apparently more God-fearing than others, as they traversed the mud between the church and the buildings. At the head of the procession was His Grace, Bishop John Craxton, the most splendidly dressed of them all, with a miter on his head and holding a crosier with a curved top made of walrus tooth. Beneath it a piece of cloth was tied, fluttering in the wind like a small banner. The boy watched in awe as the procession wound its way across the field, heard the strains of song, and soon looked down on the shaved crowns, saw them disappear into the church one by one, and then the singing was under his feet, moving further inward along the nave, alternately rising and falling, into the narthex.

Through the music his ears could make out a soft, rhythmic beat, overlapping the sounds of the mass. Hooves beating against the ground. Michael pricked up his ears like a dog, stood up, and stuck his head through the belfry window so that he could hear better. There was no mistake: it was the sound of galloping horses. He peered out into the valley, gray from the rain. There was a low-lying fog on the slopes of Mt. Holabyrda and Mt. Kalfastadahnjukur, making it hard to see. There they came, galloping out of the raw morning. Many of them, riding in a cavalcade, so fast that chunks of grassy earth were flung high into the air. They were wearing armor: iron headpieces, mail shirts. Longbows and crossbows were slung across their shoulders, swords tucked into belts, their quivers full.

Fear coursed through the boy's veins and into his consciousness. What business did men in full armor have at a synod? Were they Icelanders, or English? Or perhaps Danish, sent by the king to penalize the bishop and the rest of them for breaking the trade ban. He stared out of the window and could see the riders approaching quickly; they would catch everyone off guard unless…unless…

He did not finish the thought, just groped for the bell rope closest to him and pulled on it with all his might. The copper pendulum slammed against the body of the bell, and a mighty sound rang out, again and again. The noise was deafening. Michael let go of the rope, suddenly exhausted. His knees buckled, and he collapsed on the floor, eardrums pounding.

The singing below stopped, and anxious voices asked what in God's name was going on. From the stairs came the sound of many quick footsteps. Fortunately Hrafn was the first to reach Michael, and he immediately obeyed the boy's gesture to look outside.

"God have mercy!" he cried. The men all rushed back down and out onto the pavement. Someone called loud and clear for them to remain within the sanctity of the church. The ringing of hooves drew nearer. Dogs ran barking to greet the new arrivals. People had come out of the buildings and tents, and they were shouting, asking what was going on. In the flash of an eye, there was pure chaos: excited voices, barking, and the neighing of horses, all rolled into one.

Michael looked into the valley. They were no longer moving at a gallop but rode their horses more slowly, at a *tolt*, the gait that is unique to the Icelandic horse. They approached the yard in a long procession, two-and-two together, nearly thirty men in all.

◇◇◇

Ragna was out of the house before the ringing had stopped, checking to see what the commotion was about. Then the riders came into view. Craxton shouted for the people to go inside and bolt the doors, and for the priests to stay inside the church. Ragna happened to look up at the steeple and thought she saw a familiar face flash by. Yes, there it was again, his face filled with fear.

Oh dear Lord! Ragna crossed herself and without thinking began running across the field to the church, not stopping to wonder if her son wasn't actually safer where he was. She wanted him close to her, and she would protect him with her life if need be.

She had just got to the church doors, that by now were closed, when the men came riding up the yard. Their horses were snorting and out of breath, wet with perspiration and rain, the dogs yapping, each trying to outdo the other. She immediately recognized the two men at the front of the procession, though like many others she had already surmised who it might be: Father Jon Palsson from Grenjadarstadur and his brother Thorlakur, former butler of Holar. They were now here at the synod, no doubt having learned of the bishop's plans to remove Jon from the bountiful Grenjadarstadur vicariate and take it once more under the control of the Holar bishopric, with the help of the king's governor and most of the influential men in Thingeyjarsysla district.

She paused for a brief moment and looked at the armored men, more surprised than anything else. Who would have believed that ordained priests would call on the bishop brandishing weapons—servants of God with double-edged swords? Was this not blasphemy?

Jon Palsson, dressed in a mail shirt, bearing a sword in an ornamented sheath, and carrying a riding whip in one hand, urged his gray horse up to the church pavement. His entourage stopped a short distance away, forming a semicircle behind him.

Ragna pulled on the heavy doorknob, but it was stuck. Terrified, she pounded on the door, shouting for those inside to open in God's name.

"Oh, what bravery the residents of Holar show now, running for shelter when guests arrive and barricading the church doors to a woman in their haste." The voice was high-pitched and the tone not unfriendly. Ragna turned slowly and looked into the eyes of Father Jon Palsson, known for his poetry written to the Holy Mary, and former *officialis in spiritualibus* of the Holar bishopric. A corpulent, rotund man, he leaned forward onto the mane of his horse, his cheeks red from the ride. His iron headdress was fastened with a narrow band that almost disappeared into his double chin, and he appeared quite harmless, despite the armor.

Her fear left her. She knew that these men were not likely to harm a defenseless woman, irrespective of how they behaved toward each other. She was embarrassed that she had let them see her so afraid.

"Why do you assume they are hiding? It is mass day, as the good priest will most likely know," she replied haughtily, attempting to cover up her awkwardness. "On such days ordained men normally dress in priests' garb, not in armor, like common soldiers," she added, her courage returning.

He laughed a dry laugh, devoid of mirth. "It would not be the first time the soldiers of Christ had to defend themselves with weapons," he said. "Now kindly call the bishop."

"Call him yourself, sir," she replied snootily, unsure of where all this haughtiness came from. The twitches of a smile vanished from the priest's face. "It is like you Akrar folk to pander to English dogs and care nothing for the king's decrees or that of others as long as your own welfare is ensured, and even though he pays the lawman's wages," he said coldly and touched his whip, its handle trimmed with silver. "The young lady gave birth to an English bastard, is that not right?"

He had just finished the sentence when two things happened simultaneously. The church doors were flung open and a group of men led by the bishop came out, and a pebble came flying down as though from heaven above, straight onto the iron headdress, with such velocity that it rang out. Jon was severely alarmed and pulled hard on the reins of his stone-gray horse, which retreated backward, neighing.

One of his followers instantly placed an arrow on a crossbow and fired in the direction of the assailant in the belfry. The short metal arrow cut the air with a low whirr and landed deep in a wooden shutter that had been shut an instant before. The feathered shaft stood trembling in the wood.

John Craxton walked onto the pavement, the veins in his neck and temple swollen and his face red with agitation. He held the crosier in one hand and waved it in the direction of the priest, who was still on the back of his horse.

"How dare thee, Father Jon Palsson, add to thy earlier transgressions by coming at us with weapons?! Thou wast summoned here to answer to accusations of large-scale default on the tithes of Grenjadarstadur church, but turn up here not only as if thou wert a thief, but also as a blasphemer and invader!"

"The Lord will receive His due, as they say, and the king will receive his due. But at this time here in Iceland, the payments due to God as well as our hereditary king in Copenhagen happen to go straight into the coffers of English traders and pirates," Father Jon answered, his voice calm and steady. "I have merely withheld the tithes of Grenjadarstadur Parish at the bidding of my lord Aslak, archbishop in Nidaros, and, I might add, I have been fully within my rights in doing so. They shall be paid in the proper annates to the archbishop. I have merely ensured that they go into his hands, rather than into the vaults of the English, and thus helped ensure that our just and rightful authorities are able to strengthen the defenses of this country and maintain the trade ban. All of this has been iterated repeatedly, most recently last summer by King Henry himself."

"You would do well, Father Jon, to continue scribbling your poetry in praise of Holy Mary rather than encourage unrest against a justly appointed bishop, who is here by mandate of the pope." It was Thorkell who spoke, his demeanor arrogant. "Or is the power of Aslak Bolt in Nidaros now greater than that of Pope Martin in Rome?"

Jon Palsson looked down his narrow nose at him for an instant, seeming to judge him unworthy of an answer, and then addressed the bishop.

"Thou nurturest a serpent at thy breast, Bishop Craxton, in the person of Thorkell Gudbjartsson. That will become clear to thee as the full force of his ambition..." Father Jon broke off. No one saw exactly how it happened, but in a flash Thorkell had pulled him from the horse and flung him down into the wet grass. Men leapt out from the doors of the church, and in a heartbeat both his sword and whip had been taken. His own soldiers had no time to react except to urge their horses, yet they were instantly forced to yank on the reins since Thorkell put one knee on Jon's chest and his razor-sharp knife at his throat. The men retreated, shouting reprovals and threats at the steward of Holar, and banging halberds and pikes into their shields to add emphasis to their words. A few of the horses neighed and reared, alarmed by the excitement of their riders.

"Now both of us are on the ground, old fox, and more equal than many times before," said Thorkell through clenched teeth. "Make one move to oppose His Grace the bishop and you'll be on the road to hell before you know what's hit you!"

"The Lord will punish your soul, Thorkell Galdur of the Dark Arts," Jon groaned, speaking with difficulty after his harsh tumble. "All your curses shall turn against you."

"Do not make your humiliation worse with careless talk," Thorkell said quietly, pressing his knife a little harder against Father Jon's throat. Ragna saw a small drop trickle out from beneath the sharp blade of the knife.

"It should be perfectly clear to thee, Father Jon Palsson, and to thy entourage, that whoever rises against his bishop with threats and violence shall be subject to excommunication major on account of his actions," said Craxton. "With thy actions today, thou hast forsaken all rights to the sacrament and the company of Christian men!"

A low murmur passed among the priests and Jon's entourage, many of whom still had arrows on their bowstrings, which had been cocked when Father Jon was pulled from his horse. They now let their weapons fall, as much from surprise as from fear. They were all aware of the severity involved in this greatest punishment handed down by the church. The threat had been made many times, but it was so rarely executed that none of them could remember anyone being excommunicated in North Iceland.

Jon turned pale and stared dumbstruck at the bishop, who towered above him with his crosier raised and continued in a stronger voice: "No Christian may interact with thee at the risk of excommunication minor, with the sole exception of thy most immediate relatives. This censure shall be lifted only if thou asks for clemency with true humility. Through our generosity we shall allow thee three days to repent. We order thee to deliver to Grenjadarstadur in full the funds thou hast collected since thou unrightfully assumed office, aided by the bishop of Nidaros, and without authorization from the Holar bishopric. Should thy impenitence be such that thou disobeyest, we shall publicly read three notices to this effect, which shall be followed by full excommunication, so help us God!"

As soon as the bishop stopped speaking, the gloomy sky opened and the rain poured down in large, heavy, reproachful drops, as if to underscore his divine mandate for excommunication and denouncement.

"Release the man," Craxton said. Thorkell obeyed, placing his knife back in a sheath beneath his robe. Jon Palsson rose to his feet with some difficulty; the mail shirt was heavy on his shoulders, and the rings clattered against each other. He frowned as he cast a look at the crowd on the church pavement, looking more tired than angry. No one spoke a word; many avoided his severe gaze and looked down. Most of them had known him for years. He led his horse to a nearby hitching rock and mounted it silently, with some effort. The bishop gave a sign, and he was handed his riding whip, but not the sword.

"You shall all live to regret this," Jon declared before urging his horse and galloping down the lane, mud splashing from under its hooves. His men followed in procession, Thorlakur bringing up the rear, his wide backside rocking in the saddle. He alone looked back over his shoulder and made a threatening fist at those who stood watching them.

Ragna shivered, and she tightened her hold on her son's shoulders, who had come down from the belfry and clung to her side. She looked at Thorkell, but he seemed unfazed. He smiled.

◈

Bishop Craxton read his notices at mass over the next three days as he had announced he would. Father Jon Palsson did not come to the church to hear the bishop's words, nor did any of his representatives. No message was sent requesting reconciliation, nor were there any of repentance. Therefore on the final day of the synod, the Thursday after the feast day of St. Hallvard on May 17, it became evident that an excommunication would take place at Holar cathedral.

The rain had continued with only brief pauses, and the men's garments became nearly soaked through in the short time it took to walk in procession around the cathedral before High Mass began. The yard and the camp areas were now one large muddy expanse, having been trampled on much more than usual, and the stone floor in the church, which the female servants at Holar had tirelessly scrubbed with sand prior to the synod, was now covered in a layer of mud.

The great church was stuffed full by the time everyone was inside: the bishop, learned canons, dozens of priests from around the see, the highest-ranking men from the monasteries, nearly all the residents of Holar, and most of the parishioners. Not to mention the bishop's most highly esteemed guests of a worldly standing: Loftur the Rich Guttormsson, knight at Modruvellir, and his wife Ingibjorg Palsdottir, parents of the king's governor Ormur, with their large entourage, and many landowners from nearby districts. No one wanted to miss the excommunication, and besides, it was vital to demonstrate one's support for their bishop. The lawman at Akrar was not present, however, and only a few people from Blonduhlid. The air was thick and clammy and the church dusky, with only minimal light coming in through the stained glass in the tall, arched windows. Lighted candles in candlesticks along the walls and on the transepts on the great columns cast a flickering light over the congregation.

Mass began with the Kyrie Eleison, as usual. The bright tenor voice of Steinmodur the cantor resounded down along the nave, and when more than 120 strong-voiced priests and canons echoed the prayers, the air, infused with song, trembled. The heart of every true Christian had to be moved by the divine beauty of the song as it echoed from the dome above the altar and on throughout the entire church like the murmur of a thousand voices. The singing of the prayers gave way to psalms, and the commoners joined in, many so moved by the beauty of the music that tears welled up in their eyes, causing them to blow their noses into their fingers and on the backs of their hands. The psalm was Kolbeinn Tumason's "Hear, Thou Maker of Heaven" in Nordic, and some grinned to themselves, recalling that the composer of the psalm had himself been excommunicated by Gvendur, bishop of Holar, some two centuries earlier, something of which the foreign Bishop Craxton was likely unaware.

From the lectorium Father Thorkell intoned the sermon from the First Epistle of Peter, chapter five, in a deep voice, so that both high and low might hear the Word of God: *"Be sober, be vigilant; because your adversary the devil, as a roaring lion, walketh about, seeking whom he may devour: Resist him, stedfast in the faith."* When the final note had sounded, there was silence for a few moments, after which bells began to ring and a murmur passed through the congregation: It was time!

The churchgoers who stood at the back, closest to the door, tried to elbow their way closer in to have a better view, but the overcrowding was such that it was difficult to see what took place next to the holy of all holies, except for those who stood next to the choir doors. Michael was among them; he had slipped in front of the men-servants, schoolboys, and farmers, one by one, lithe as a cat, and now he had a fine view into the bright choir, where thick wax candles shone in the hands of the priests. In front of the beautifully carved bishop's throne, His Grace John Williamsson Craxton stood with a burning candle in his raised hands and began to sing in Latin. The meaning eluded Michael— Latin was not his strong suit—but he was sure that this was the excommunication itself, *excommunicatio maior.* Those were the words that barred Father Jon Palsson of Grenjadarstadur Parish from all the sacraments of the holy church, thereby condemning him to eternal hell and damnation if he did not repent and serve true penance within the time decreed. For those who were excommunicated from the church, the gate to heaven was locked. A shiver ran down the boy's back.

Now twelve clerics came and arranged themselves in a semicircle on either side of the bishop, each representing one of Christ's apostles. Each had the flickering light of life and blessings, shining on the candles they held in extended hands. The flames danced to and fro in the draft, illuminating the grave countenances of those assembled with an unsteady light. Craxton stepped out among them and threw his candle on the floor, and in a loud voice he proclaimed: "Thy light shall be extinguished in this manner, Jon Palsson, for all eternity!" The priests quickly followed suit and threw their candles onto the stone floor, responding in unison: "Amen! Amen!" The candles rolled around and collided; some went out immediately, while others glowed until the priests came forward and stepped on the wicks until the flames were completely extinguished. At that, darkness descended on the choir of Holar cathedral.

Father Jon Palsson had now been cast into a dark world of sin and torment. And Grenjadarstadur Parish was free to be handed over to his successor.

"Why won't you come with me? You would be in charge of the entire household at Grenjadarstadur and would live as my wife in every way, except in name. Foreign bishops may not have an understanding for this, but you know as well as I do that Icelanders are used to priests having mistresses." Thorkell spoke kindly and convincingly, yet she felt her obstinacy rise up within her. She could not agree to his proposal.

"You betrayed me," she said curtly. The words slipped out, and she instantly felt childish and ashamed. She could have asked him, rather than snap at him like that. What if he didn't protest? She dug her fingernails into her palms and stared at the floor to prevent him from melting the sheet of ice in her heart with his eyes. The silence became intolerably long.

"No," he said after an eternity. Too long. He took both of her hands in his and pulled her to him.

"You alone have my heart. Other women mean nothing to me, and never have. All they have done is given me help to release those urges that are natural to a man." Thorkell removed the comb that held up the thick braid in the nape of her neck, and he separated her black hair with his long, white fingers.

Ragna leaned against his chest and closed her eyes, listening to the beating of his heart. Then she pulled herself together, took a deep breath, put her flat palm on his chest, and pushed him away.

"I cannot leave. I manage the household, I am in charge of people who look up to me and trust me." Perhaps not everyone, not anymore. "Bishop Craxton relies on me. I have caused enough disgrace to my parents. The bishop's friendship and respect are very important to my people. And Michael needs to stay in school. It would be an offense to the bishop, who has withdrawn his tuition fees, to remove him. Other parents must pay the equivalent of many heads of cattle and even large pieces of land to educate and board their sons here. My son can claim no inheritance or anything else, but if he is allowed to continue his education and enjoys the favor of the bishop, he might even become a priest. I must think of others."

She spoke rapidly so that he would not interrupt her, the words spilling out. "You know how it would look if I went with you, Thorkell. People might not care, but they would know, and they would laugh behind our backs. I don't want to go. I cannot sacrifice everything I have worked for here."

"I thought you were courageous, Ragna," he said. "It takes courage to love, and it takes love to forgive." He threw up his hands in resignation. "You are not the woman I thought you were. I thought you would be happy to be free. I cannot understand your thinking, cannot understand that you don't want to be free from Craxton's tyranny, he who watches everything and everyone here during every waking moment."

"I don't feel like I have him breathing down my neck, apart from that which he is perfectly entitled to with his domestics," she said, annoyed on Craxton's behalf, but mostly to refute Thorkell. Who was he to accuse her of cowardice? "It would be worse if the bishop did not observe what goes on here and record it."

"Oh yes, that would be terrible," answered Thorkell scornfully. "Icelanders might earn a noble or two were it not for the strong hand of John Craxton, who manages everything so skillfully for the merchants in King's Lynn and Bristol."

"What are you saying?" she asked, astonished. "Do you and Jon Palsson actually concur, after everything that has happened?! Did you not say to me, and agree with my foster-father in that regard, that the English should be free to trade here? Did you not say that the Danish have no mandate to prevent trade with them while they have not honored signed contracts regarding sea voyages to this country?"

"These are matters too complex for the female mind," he said, although his manner was softer than before. "Of course I want the English to be able to trade with us. I want anyone to be able to trade with us, and for the fish to go to those who offer the highest price. Don't you see, silly woman, that as long as one nation has a monopoly on trade, the price gets pushed down and profits pile up in coffers on the other side of the sea. In such cases it makes no difference whether it goes into the coffers of kings and merchants in Denmark, Norway, Lübeck, or England. Gold nobles that rightfully belong to us Icelanders are taken from the country and given to those whom the pope has the greatest interest in supporting at any given time. King Henry of England, King Eric of Pommern, Archbishop Aslak in Nidaros…they all want to get rich off Icelandic resources." He spoke fast and lowered his voice, even though he had locked the door to the office behind them. "Or can you tell me what it matters to us whether the bishop is an English pope's man like John Craxton, or a Danish king's man like Jon Gerreksson Furhat in the Skalholt see in South Iceland, who surrounds himself with an army of thugs who go around robbing and plundering in this country?!" He did not wait for an answer and was now so excited that she recoiled, slightly alarmed. "None, I tell you! It does not change a damn thing. They treat us like puppets in the name of God, the pope, and the king, but the only thing that is holy to them is the silver they collect for themselves and their masters in foreign lands. And we stay behind, impoverished beggars, humiliated, idiotic, and stupid."

"It's almost like you aspire to be bishop yourself." She said it half-jokingly, finding his passion a little daunting, but when she saw his expression, she realized that maybe she had it exactly right.

"There has not been an Icelandic bishop at Holar for nearly a century," he said, "whereas in the past there were many."

"Then wouldn't you need to ride to Rome, rather than Grenjadarstadur?" she asked. She enjoyed provoking him. What lofty ideas he had about himself!

He seemed not to catch her sarcasm; his gaze was distant, almost as though he were trying to see the future.

"Those who control the fish trade tell the pope whom to appoint. Observing Lent calls for vast stores of stockfish..." Thorkell stopped, briefly thoughtful. Then he seemed to return to his normal self. He laughed and grasped her waist tightly.

"Ah, but I should not speak of such things with a woman. Come to Grenjadarstadur with me, Ragna. I'll teach your boy myself. Stop your stubbornness. You care for me and you cannot change that, even if you are upset about Gudrun right now. It will pass."

"Don't belittle me or my thoughts," she said drily and removed his hands from her waist. "I don't like it."

"What do you want from me?" he said harshly. "Do you want me to prostrate myself before you, to beg your forgiveness?"

She made no answer, just moved toward the door. The key was in the lock. Before she could reach it, Thorkell was standing in her way.

"All right," he said tenderly, "I beg you. I love you like no man ever will. Come away with me. Let's stand together and show them what we are capable of."

"A priest's concubine is not capable of anything," she answered curtly. "Let me pass!" She pushed him from the door and tried to turn the key with trembling hands, but without success.

"Is this how we shall say good-bye, dearest Ragna?"

She did not answer, just worked the key in the door until it opened.

"I have work to do," she said. She was about to leave, but he slammed the door, close to her face, and held it closed.

"You're one to talk of betrayal," he said, and was angry again. "You, who betrayed my trust, your son a living and perpetual reminder of my humiliation."

She gasped for air. "Your humiliation?! How dare you…" At a loss for words, she raised her hand to slap him in the face, but he caught her wrist. In his eyes she saw all that remained unsaid and of which they had never spoken. At that moment she realized that his pain was no less real than hers. It was because of her that he had become a priest. He would have become a leader among chieftains had not everything turned out differently than intended.

"Stop," she begged.

But Thorkell Gudbjartsson had kept quiet long enough.

"Every single vagabond makes a meal out of that story. Oh yes, it is a tasty morsel for the beggars of this country. They get meat and dried fish for telling whoever cares to listen how my betrothed let a shipwrecked and pathetic English sailor knock her up. They also say he was unconscious at the time, so he must have needed quite a bit of help."

"I was only a child." He voice was tearful. "I had no idea…"

"No idea?!" He shook his head. "Oh, you had an idea, already fourteen winters old, how children are made. Stop lying, Ragna. You have flaws, just like everyone else."

"How cruel you are. How can you claim to love me if that is what you think of me?"

"Because that's how it is." Thorkell walked away from her, sighing deeply. "Our paths will run alongside each other, no matter how we oppose the will of our creator."

She did not argue. She felt as though she knew nothing anymore, neither God's will nor her own.

"I will not go," she said softly, and slipped through the door.

❖

He left without saying good-bye. I watched him go, looked out through the glass in the great hall at them riding down the valley, five together, each leading two horses and packhorses in a train. Gudrun stood on the front step with the girl bawling into her apron. Am I self-centered and cruel because I will not forgive? I look at them, poor and destitute, and feel angry and sad at the same time. Her belly is rapidly expanding. Damn him, that he will not take her with him! And yet I am relieved. And then once again doubtful. Should I have done what he asked of me? I cannot trust him. One moment he is loving and kind, the next wild and intense. The darkness in his eyes frightens me, as though it might swallow me up if I am not careful. It takes courage to love, he said. It is hard to be courageous when you know that no one can be trusted, least of all your loved one. No one but yourself, and perhaps the holy mother of God. It also takes courage to continue living as though nothing has changed when your lover has betrayed you, either with another person or by leaving. When all is said and done, there is not such a vast difference. Perhaps it is worse to see your loved one thirst for life every day while you would rather die from misery and grief but must go on living, if only for your child. And thereby die on the inside, again and again.

SIGNS FROM ABOVE

Summer finally arrived at the outer edge of the world, and the cows were set free from the cowshed. They sprinted over the fields, wildly elated, bucking their behinds and mooing while they rolled in the dew. Nearly every day and night was warm and sunny. The sky over Skagafjord was bluer than in other parts of the world during those brilliant June nights. It was even warm when it rained, and you could almost hear the moist grass sprouting.

The summer brought English ships, which fished off the coast. Icelanders who only owned small boats and bobbed around near the shore were stricken with envy as the English pulled cod in abundance from the sea and laid it in salt. They were still keen to buy stockfish, but they wanted to pay less than before. Consequently, men came to Holar with increasing frequency to air their disputes and complaints, and to ask His Grace John Williamsson Craxton to mediate. The proper course of action in such cases would have been to consult with the magistrate or lawman, but the bishop had a better way with the English and was moreover relatively fair—for an Englishman, at least. It also happened to be to his advantage to negotiate a decent price, for he also traded with his countrymen, buying from them malt and flour, honey and wax, and paying them in stockfish that the farmers paid to the see in the form of tithes.

For this reason and others, there was a steady flow of people to Holar, usually Icelanders, but sometimes also foreigners, wealthy persons as well as charity recipients, traders, and farmers. There were fewer vagabonds than frequently in the past as there was work aplenty for all able-bodied persons, and the English were even beginning to hire Icelanders for work, much to the chagrin of the landowners. However, as usual there was a crowd gathered at the Feast of St. Olaf, at the beginning of the hay season, to receive the alms that on that day were distributed with more generosity than on regular days. The needy and poor took it upon themselves to travel a vast distance on foot; while they were there, they could pray to merciful Mary in the cathedral. They would ask Her to care for them a bit better that year, preferably better than last year, and would light a tallow candle in front of the gentle icon, the most beautiful in all of North Iceland, and even the entire country.

Ragna was in charge of the handouts, the food stores and pantry being her responsibility. Having not been involved in this work in the past, it alarmed her to see how many needy there were, and how many of them were disabled from birth or due to illness. She found it hardest to see the lepers, for not only did they suffer from their disease, they were also outcast and condemned to be all alone until the bitter end, having no refuge except perhaps in the abbey hospitals. Even the homes of their own families were closed to them, in spite of the common belief that the cause of the illness lay with the parents of the poor wretches, since the children had most likely been conceived during a major holy day, or on a Sunday, or—worse—while the mother was menstruating. Charitable offerings for the lepers were normally placed on a tussock some distance from the houses, where they could fetch them. These offerings were normally quite generous, as the benefactors felt guilty about their overwhelming fear of the recipients, and they attempted in this way to make restitution for their own health and well being.

Ragna recognized the odd beneficiary, usually one who had managed to eke out a living by begging for many years, and who in return related news from other districts, recited poetry, and conferred God's blessings upon the givers. Thus she sometimes received the first accounts of what happened in the nearby districts and related some of them to Father Ari Thorbjarnarson, who now held the post of *officialis* in place of Thorkell. He, in turn, told the bishop, who made a point of keeping up with events. Some things that reached her ears she did not repeat, assuming that Craxton would hear of them through other, speedier, channels. One such was the rumor that Thorkell had collected goods from an English vessel that was wrecked near Hardbakur at Sletta and had either sold them for a modest price or given them away throughout the Thingeyjarthing district, to people who had been wronged in their dealings with the English.

"Those people who wanted to condemn Father Jon Palsson for forbidding them from harvesting sulphur got the best bits," said the old woman who told the story, and she lifted the muddy hem of her skirt, satisfied. She wore new and sturdy English shoes made of dark cowhide, laced, with a band across the top of the foot. "But still, Father Thorkell will not allow anyone to sell sulphur to the English. He has it transported to Grenjadarstadur and says it should go toward paying Father Jon's debts, but no one knows what he plans to do with the sulphur there, except perchance to sell it for a much higher price than people usually get and thereby earn as much as possible for the bishop."

"Perhaps," Ragna answered calmly, as if she were indifferent to the news. Yet her heart was heavy. What was Thorkell up to? To claim for himself flotsam that was the rightful property of the Holar church was bad enough, but that he should let it become known was an odd strategy and hardly one that would serve him well.

❖

The woman with the wide hips and ample bosom was neither old nor young. Her back showed the beginnings of a hump, her posture was stooped, and she had gray bristly hair that was gathered in a thick bun at the nape of her neck. Her garments were worn and patched and gave the definite impression that they were the only ones she owned. She said her name was Gudridur Aladottir and she was looking for employment.

"My dear Gvendur died a week after Midsummer Day. His heart stopped beating from sorrow, and it is no wonder, considering all that has happened since our Brynhildur was taken from us last year," she said. "The housekeeper may think it strange for me to come to the place that has claimed both her and the few heads of sheep that we owned, but I see no other way to clear our debt. I can barely earn enough to feed myself on account of the hump, and will hardly be able to scrape by on my own. But though I am no longer of much use, I cannot believe that the bishop will send me to live my life as a vagrant, knowing the tribulations that I have been subjected to by the Lord."

"Bishop Craxton does not send anyone away into such a life," said Ragna, hoping she was right. "I will take you to the bishop myself. His Grace is most likely in the great hall at this time of day, which as it happens is the best time to speak with him."

Gudridur curtsied. "It would mean a great deal to me if the housekeeper would be kind enough to first show me where my Brynka is buried. I believe she is outside the churchyard…"

Ragna wrapped a thick woolen shawl over her shoulders and walked with her down the yard and to the northern end of the churchyard. There was a cool breeze, and she shivered.

"Six children I lost young to paradise, and now another six have been sent to strangers throughout the district, all because of her, the scoundrel," said Gudridur, bitter. She looked at her daughter's grave with dry eyes and made the sign of the cross over it in the name of the Lord with a work-weary hand. "How can one forgive something like that, and how can one not? She was my own flesh and blood, and always good to her little siblings. And now she is in eternal damnation. It has even been said that she did not lie still in her grave this past winter."

Ragna hesitated. "She received a requiem from an ordained priest," she said quietly. "I am sure that she rests in peace...now, at least."

Gudridur looked at her, astonished. "What did you say? Who was the merciful soul?"

"I cannot tell you, and I beg you not to tell anyone. The gesture is the same, regardless."

Gudridur nodded. "To be sure, and may God bless the man and forgive him, and my Brynhildur, too." Her eyes grew moist, and she blew her nose on her patched sleeve.

Yet her courage failed her completely when they were ushered into the great hall and her eyes took in the curtains with gold stitching and tapestries on every wall, writing desks and carved benches bolstered with brocade and plush, gold candle holders on the bishop's table, and gold-trimmed caskets that could have contained the finger bone of a saint or even a wooden splinter from the cross of the Savior. The old woman sank to her knees, overcome with humility, and kissed the bishop's purple cloak hem instead of the ring that he extended toward her, stammering "May the peace of God be with you" and entreating Holy Mary to help her. A smiling Craxton raised her up and asked her to sit down on a bench, despite her own reluctance, saying that he was merely one of Christ's most humble brothers, being of the order of Saint Francis, who gave away all his belongings and lived by the mercy of God and the charity of men.

"Just like you, dear mother," he said in his strange foreign accent, sat down in an elaborately carved chair, and looked inquisitively at Ragna. The woman was downcast, stared at the floor, and said nothing other than what might be interpreted as prayers. Her expression was restless and anguished, as is common among those who have lost most of their children to the grave, or to strangers, or both.

"What is it that the housekeeper feels warrants our attention on this day?"

"This woman is the mother of Brynhildur Gudmundsdottir," Ragna replied. "She has lost her husband, her livestock has been sold, and her children have been sent to foster homes."

The bishop frowned. "Brynhildur?" he asked. Then it was as though it dawned on him. "Ah, the servant girl who ran away and they had already taken out her salary and…" He stopped mid-sentence, slightly uncomfortable.

"She is a hard worker and is offering to work off the rest of the debt."

Ragna placed her hands over Gudridur's shoulders, as if to draw attention away from her hump. The woman stooped even more.

"What do the books tell us about her debt to the Holar bishopric, good notary?" Craxton addressed his scribe, Jon Egilsson, a thin man with a convex nose and a sharp gaze. The notary deftly pulled out a large vellum book and flipped carefully through its densely written pages until he found what he was looking for.

"Brynhildur Gudmundsdottir shall pay a fine of thirty marks, and her parents fifteen," he read, his voice slightly nasal. His tongue, sticking out from the corner of his mouth, was black from a long habit of sticking the end of the quill into his mouth to wet it before he started writing. "The debt shall be paid in the coins of the realm prior to the end of service; otherwise, it will be deducted from Brynhildur's salary, et cetera." He flipped through a few additional pages, running his finger down the columns. "The parents have completed their payments; in arrears are…thirty marks." He closed the book.

Gudridur was still downcast, staring at the floor. She whispered something, and Ragna leaned forward to hear better.

"She says she still owes the parish priest for her husband's funeral service."

The bishop reached into his pocket and took out a silver coin that he handed to the woman.

"Dear mother, your debt has been paid in tears and grief, and here is silver to pay the priest. You will perform the tasks that the housekeeper gives you and receive the appropriate remuneration for your service."

"May God reward Your Grace," Gudridur whispered, rolling the coin between her fingers. On one side there were imprinted letters that she could not understand, and on the other a profile of a clean-shaven man with a straight nose, his hair cut in a line parallel to his ears. His expression denoted a very important personage. "Is this perchance His Highness the King?"

Craxton nodded. "It is His Royal Highness King Henry the Fifth of England."

"Is the English king our monarch now?" asked Gudridur, astonished, albeit not intending to offend her benefactor.

Craxton gave a forced smile. "Ah, no, dear mother. Yet he is more kindly disposed toward the Icelanders than the one who now reigns over the Kalmar Union of Scandinavia and seeks to bring down his own subjects for the sole cause of trading with the English. And this even though all other trade is out of the question due to his own war with merchants of the Hanseatic League. Bergen is reported to be in ruins as a result." He cleared his throat and looked at Jon the scribe, who was in the process of writing the most current entry into the debt registry. "Escort the woman to the kitchen, my good man, and leave me and the housekeeper alone for a bit. I must speak with her privately."

The notary laid down his quill and obeyed without a word. Gudridur was more bold than when she first arrived, being now a debt-free woman, and she gave only a half-curtsy when she left. Ragna felt a growing unease; what could the bishop wish to discuss with her that he thought right to hide from the scribe, his closest associate—unless it was that which must be hidden from all men, particularly him.

"It concerns Thorkell Gudbjartsson," the bishop said as the doors closed behind the scribe and Gudridur, and Ragna had obeyed his gesture to perch on a stool opposite him.

A small cry escaped her lips. She instantly covered her mouth and faked a cough, hoping she could prevent Craxton from noticing her alarm, muttering something about the soot in the air. Concerned, he poured some ale into a goblet and handed it to her.

"I hope you are not catching an infection, Cousin," he said amiably. She shook her head and sipped on the ale, then realized what he had said, and frowned:

"Cousin? Why do you address me in that way, Bishop Craxton?"

"Yes, you heard right," he said, smiling. "I am told by Father Steinmodur, who is familiar with all lineages here in the north, that your mother's great-grandfather hailed from Gudbrandsdalur Valley in Norway, just like my entire maternal lineage."

Ragna had no other response to this astonishing information but to smile with relief; he was unlikely to reprimand her if their newly discovered affiliation was at the forefront of his mind. "And now, please, call me Jon Vilhjalmsson according to the Nordic tradition. You know I prefer that name," he added, with a hint of impatience.

"Mr. Jon Vilhjalmsson," she said and lowered her head in humility.

The bishop gave a perfunctory smile, then frowned once more. "I am concerned about Thorkell," he said. "I have heard talk of him riding through the countryside with a group of armed men at his side, and that a few days ago his band was in a dispute with the crew from the balinger *Bartholomew* from King's Lynn. Men were wounded in that conflict, both Icelandic and English, but none were slain, praise God. In my short time in this country, it has already come to pass that a priest has taken up arms against me and has refused to seek reconciliation despite this leading to his excommunication. I wonder if I might expect another to do the same." He was quiet for a few moments and looked at her with an ambiguous expression, then continued. "I know that you and Father Thorkell are good friends. And that is why I ask, and you have my full confidence, as I have yours: What is his purpose, and why on earth has he not sought the help of the Holar see after such events?"

Ragna was taken aback. "I was not aware of this danger; I can hardly believe it," she said, and added a moment later, "Is it absolutely certain that Father Thorkell was involved?"

"I have had credible reports that he was involved in the altercation along with his band of men, though it is not sure whether he was the perpetrator," the bishop answered. "I am the first to admit that my countrymen are not all men of refinement, and there are even some who have sought employment on vessels bound for Iceland because they were pursued at home as a result of their aggression and violence. Be that as it may, it is highly inappropriate, and indeed strictly forbidden, for a man of God to ride armed throughout the provinces and take the country's defense into his own hands."

"This clash must have sprung from an emergency, that Thorkell will surely be able to explain. Could it not be that injuries have prevented his journey here, rather than unwillingness?"

"Maybe, maybe." The bishop drummed his fingers on the carved arms of the chair, clearly not satisfied. "However, in that case he could have sent a man with a letter. I have sent him two this summer, neither of which he has seen fit to answer. I have been going over his account entries from earlier years, and there are shortcomings. I believed he was one of the few men who could be trusted, but now I no longer know what to believe." He grasped the arms of the chair and leaned forward, looking intently into Ragna's eyes. "Do you think it likely that he will join forces with Jon Palsson, who is said to be gathering forces in Oxarfjord, in the north?"

"No, not likely at all," Ragna answered without hesitation. "You can be sure that he would never do that." She was relieved that she could answer truthfully in that respect, though other things would have to remain unsaid. "I would be inclined to believe that he had armed his men to go against Jon Palsson's forces, that is how strong their acrimony is," she added.

"You are quite certain of that?" The bishop leaned back against the cushions once more and peered with his slate-gray eyes, like he wished to see through her. "I do hope you are right. What have you heard from Thorkell since he left? You must have received some news of him?"

She shook her head, somewhat uncomfortable. "Nothing more than the stories the vagrants carry from farm to farm, which are rarely credible."

"Such as?"

Ragna fidgeted and avoided his sharp gaze. "There is some talk about him not having delivered flotsam that was found north of Sletta, and some say that he is a bit too harsh when it comes to collecting what Father Jon owes the see. But for that he has Your Grace's permission and orders, isn't that so?"

"Yes, that is correct." The bishop was quiet for a good while, lost in thought. For a moment she thought that surely he could read her mind and all those things that were unsaid, but she shook off the notion. What did she know of Thorkell's intentions, if any? His grandiose talk was probably just that—talk.

"I expect you to tell me immediately if and when you receive further news of him, and especially if you hear from him personally. I repeat that you have my full confidence." He smiled at her, that ambiguous smile, and she understood that the conversation was over. She stood up.

That same instant there was a light knock on the door and Jon Egilsson the notary returned. He bowed deeply and respectfully to Ragna as she left the room. When he straightened up, their eyes met; his knowledge was evident in his eyes, and she shivered.

◆

In mid-August, shortly after the Feast of St. Mary, Father Jon Palsson arrived at Holar along with Asbjorn, abbot of the Thingeyrar monastery. A dozen men made up their entourage. The abbot had arranged a reconciliatory meeting, even though the demeanor and countenances of the men did not suggest a great desire for harmony. Indeed, they seemed more interested in fighting, for apart from the two who were ordained, all were fully armed. Swords and knives gleamed beneath cloaks and coats, and little was done to conceal the weapons. No clouds obscured the hot August sunshine, and drops of perspiration glistened on the brows of the men. The horses flicked their tails in an ineffective attempt to cool themselves in the humidity and drive away the flies. The late summer had been unusually warm, and barely a drop of rain had fallen for weeks.

The Holar clerks stood in a cluster on the terrace and shifted awkwardly. Finally the newly appointed steward, Father Ari, stepped forward and asked the men in a trembling voice to lay their weapons beneath the church wall before entering the great hall for the meeting, and not to commit further sins against His Grace the bishop by doubting his sincere desire to negotiate and reconcile. The abbot immediately echoed this earnest wish. After a brief hesitation and a gesture from Father Jon, the men dismounted, took their arms, and laid them in a pile on the pavement. Two of them remained next to the pile; the others walked into the cool shade of the great hall to meet with His Grace Bishop Craxton.

The meeting was short, lasting barely an hour, and when Jon Palsson came striding out, he was fuming, his face dark red with agitation. Not only had the bishop demanded that he give back to the holy see of Holar the two lands that were his rightful property,

constituting wages for the years that he had been steward following the death of Bishop Jon Tofason, he had also wanted twenty
head of cattle as penance. On top of all else, he had flatly refused
to reinstall Father Jon at Grenjadarstadur, even if the debt was
paid. The chapter had already ruled and reiterated that the Holar
see was in charge of appointments for that parish, and not the
archbishop in Nidaros.

"Such a great price I shall not pay for indulgence and forgiveness," Jon Palsson shouted, slamming his fist on the table. And
so there was no repentance and no reconciliation, and nothing
remained behind but the large cloud of dust that trailed Father
Jon and his men as they galloped down the Holar yard and out
along Hjaltadalur Valley.

◈

A few days later, a new group of visitors arrived at the Holar
bishopric. There were twenty of them together, apt horsemen,
but clearly tired. One of them lay slouched and dazed across the
mane of his horse, which was led by one of his cohorts. Their garments and dark, weathered appearance suggested that they were
English sailors, and the harsh manner of the two men who led the
procession indicated that those two were a rank above the rest.
The locals made a point of moving out of their way, mistrustful
and some of them fearful. Rumors of conflict between English
sailors and the men of Grenjadarstadur had passed throughout
the country, and the new arrivals all had long daggers in their
belts, or longbows and quivers over their shoulders. They carried a large chest with supplies and two barrels of ale, but they
allowed no one to come near to help unpack the horses, nor did
they seem likely to offer anything for sale.

The two who appeared to lead the group, a bowlegged captain and a merchant with a callous look in his eyes, disappeared into the great hall to meet with the bishop, while the rest of the men lay flat on the sloping grass and refused offers to step inside. They kept their horses with them and would accept nothing but ale, which Ragna had brought to them. The one who appeared the weakest had a bloody bandage tied around his right arm and appeared more dead than alive, his eyes burning with fever. Ragna ignored the objections of the men and had farmhands support him into the quarters that held bedridden elders and the ill. As soon as he was laid in a bed, the man lost consciousness, surrounded by curious servants and old people who groped their way onto the edges of the beds to catch a glimpse of the foreigner.

When the dirty linen bandages, suffused with coagulated blood, were removed, such a stench rose up that everyone around began to retch and fled the premises, one by one. Finally only Ragna and an elderly woman known as Herbal-Anna remained behind to administer to the man. The wound was large, clearly from a blow, and was partially closed by a bloody scab. It oozed putrid, greenish pus.

"Some say that the secretions are the best thing for removing evil from the body and stopping the purulence, but in my experience it is best to remove it and then burn the place from whence the foulness oozes, for otherwise it will never close," said Herbal-Anna and handed Ragna a damp cloth. "Wipe him clean while I heat a blade for burning and put together a poultice to apply to the sore."

Ragna obeyed, holding her nose, as the stench was overpowering. The man mumbled something incoherent, tossed and turned, and opened his eyes wide, terrified in his delirium. She shushed him and hummed soothingly, which seemed to work since he stopped mumbling, closed his eyes, and lay still while she finished cleaning the filth from the wound. Herbal-Anna put a pot on the hearth, into which she threw her medicinal herbs, reciting the Lord's Prayer and something else that perhaps was not quite as Christian, while Ragna sat on the side of the Englishman's bed and washed his face and his calloused hands. She pulled off his darned, grimy togs and could not help but think back in time. She even felt as though there was a resemblance between them, this wounded sailor and her Michael, but she wasn't sure whether it was just the black hair and brown eyes. Michael's countenance had long since been obliterated from her memory, but the recollection of his toned, sinewy body still lived within her.

Had the Englishman been remotely conscious before, that state was completely obliterated when Herbal-Anna arrived with a red-hot knife blade just taken from the fire, and with pincers placed it swiftly on the open wound. The man bucked to one side with a heavy groan and then lay still. The stench of burnt flesh filled their nostrils. She then applied the hot compress firmly over the entire wound and wound a linen bandage tightly around it, talking incessantly to the unconscious sailor, Ragna, and herself, all at the same time, asking why on earth the English were engaged in brawls with upright persons and what sort of dreadful times these were that they could not even keep peace with God's ordained men, to say nothing of others. And now there was talk once more of children being abducted, and still no sign of those poor bairns that the new bishop in Skalholt had made the English promise to release and return from slavery in England. Ragna said little, and she was not surprised as to how well-informed the herbalist was about these events, since those who sought her services were all plagued by some illness, and in return for healing sorrel for their wounds and juniper berries and angelica and caraway seeds for their headaches or toothaches, she received all the tidings that could be passed on. No doubt those who had few reports simply made things up, or at the very least exaggerated them.

But Herbal-Anna proved to be right about the sailors having been wounded in a brawl with the men of Grenjadarstadur. They were from the vessel *Bartholomew* from King's Lynn and had come to Holar to make peace with the Icelanders and to seek strategic advice from the bishop, since he was one of the few men who understood their language to any useful degree, as well as their cause. After talks behind closed doors in the great hall, it was decided that the English would be given sole occupancy of the guest quarters. They were just as mistrustful as the locals, and wanted to be able to lock the doors at night, despite the bishop's assurances that no one would touch a hair on the head of any of the overnight guests at Holar.

Craxton had the Englishmen seated at his own high table at supper, along with the Holar priests and others who were proficient in English. Little was said at first, neither by the Icelanders nor the foreigners, but as the eating went on and toasts had been drunk to all the relevant holy personages, they became more talkative. Gradually their dispositions grew more amiable from the strong mead and tender lamb.

Ragna served the bishop's table as usual, along with two female servants, and the men kept them on their toes. The English greedily imbibed the meat, laughing and remarking that from spring until fall they rarely received other freshly caught food than the fish that they drew from the sea. Consequently they were weak—and virtually ill—from shortage of meat.

In the kitchen, the servant girls whispered among themselves about the excesses they observed, and they were mildly indignant about the hospitality and generosity shown by His Grace the bishop toward the men who had accosted his own priest and friend. Moreover, it was now being said that they had harmed upright farmers in Thingeyjarsysla—unless that had been sailors from another vessel. At any rate, they were nothing more than English thugs, each and every one of them. That the bishop should have promised them protection they found incomprehensible—that is, until one of the girls claimed to have heard Jon the notary say that the sailors planned to sell a half-share in their seagoing vessel in return for the see's current supplies of stockfish, which nonetheless amounted to only about twelve ship holds.

Ragna did not scold them for gossiping, nor did she join in, any more than was her custom. On the other hand, she was filled with resentment about Craxton's servile reception of his countrymen. What was he thinking, provoking everyone around him in this way? Later that evening, wagging tongues in the kitchen grew considerably more kindly, since the English compensated each and every girl who had served at table generously with a silver coin. They then went and fetched the chest they had brought with them, taking from it a large wooden box that they placed in the middle of the dining hall floor. Upon the boards being removed, a winged alabaster altarpiece appeared, adorned with low reliefs so beautifully painted and decorated that a hush fell on the crowd. The flustered priests rubbed their hands together in pleasure and gratitude. In the middle of the altarpiece, the deity sat on a throne, dressed in a ruby red cloak, with the crucified Christ in front of him and a white dove above. On either side of them were the archangels Michael and Raphael, holding a blue sky over God the Father, decorated with gold stars.

The bishop beamed and thanked the Englishmen for this magnanimous gift to Holar cathedral, which as well as serving as praise to God was also meant to be an offering of repentance. As a result of provocation and misunderstanding, the crew had clashed with the priest at Grenjadarstadur, Father Thorkell Gudbjartsson, and had injured him and some of his men.

Ragna inhaled sharply at those last words, and she came dangerously close to crying out in anger. How dare Craxton provide indulgence for a fee, for practically the same cause that had led to the excommunication of Jon Palsson? Greater cause, in fact, for there had been no bloodshed, except in Jon's own case, even if it was only a drop.

"How seriously may one injure an ordained man and still be absolved by such an expensive altarpiece?" she asked coldly.

The bishop raised his eyebrows. "Thy behavior is inappropriate, good housekeeper," he said calmly but decisively. "Thou shouldst consider the decorum of thy position and not involve thyself in matters that do not concern thee."

She was speechless with emotion and could only turn and flee the room, cheeks burning. She nearly tripped on the hem of her skirt as she turned away from the guests who sat, speechless, at the tables.

"Are you deranged!?" the incredulous servant girls asked as they followed her into the kitchen. "Has there ever been a more valued treasure than that altarpiece, and you ask how many men they are allowed to hurt for it?"

Ragna pushed them away impatiently, without answering. She could not endure their cackling voices and felt like she was suffocating from the air in the kitchen, thick with soot and smoke and the heavy smell of meat. She hurried outside. The August evening was warm and fair, and it calmed her to breathe in the clear air and the silence.

She wandered aimlessly into the dung-scented dusk, away from the buildings, down to the church, and along the church-yard wall. Just north of the yard, she came to Brynhildur's grave. She stopped there and knelt down. Someone had planted a flea-bane in front of the little wooden cross. Her mother, no doubt. Wild mayweed grew all around. Ragna lay down in the dewy grass next to Brynhildur, reached out her arms like Christ on the cross, and looked up at the heavens. In the eastern sky, there was a full moon, and the stars twinkled in the far distance.

❖

How serious are Thorkell's injuries? Does he ever think of me? Will we meet again soon? Should I have forgiven him? Followed him? Would these events have come to pass if I had? Useless thoughts. All that has come to pass will not be changed, and in no way can I influence that which is yet to happen. Everything is in God's hands, and resisting His will can only come to harm. Yet how can I know for certain what is God's will? Perhaps it was always His intention that Thorkell and I would be one. Perhaps I was sent to Holar for that very reason. To fix what went wrong. It is strange, but I now find it matters more than anything to me that he be safe, even more than the fact that he betrayed me.

❖

As she lay there, outstretched, staring at the moon, it began to change before her eyes. Its bright, yellow-white surface grew darker and more rosy, and after a short while it was blood-red,

112

almost the color of the sun when it sets at the end of the day. It shone a maroon light into the dusky mantle of the evening. At first she believed this curious shading was no more than a figment of her own imagination, and she did not move, merely admired its beauty. She felt her own insignificance in the Lord's creation, her arms still outstretched like she was embracing the vastness of space. It was not until the minutes ticked by and the burgundy moon began to turn brighter once more that she realized that it had not been her own imagination. She began to grow apprehensive, and then fear seized her completely. Surely such a strange vision was a sign of terrible events to come—bloodshed and death.

Slowly Ragna drew her arms toward her body and laid them protectively over her chest. She felt the hard ground beneath her and the moisture that in places had seeped through the linen of her dress. The moon gradually returned to its normal state, though it retained a rosy hue in its shadows and outer edges for a moment. A dog howled somewhere in the distance, lonely and frightened of the unknown, just like her.

A chill passed through her and she stood up, brushed off her skirts, and walked quickly back to the houses. She was not sure how long she had been gone—her sense of passing time had vanished in the dark—but she saw in the faint green glimmer that shone through the small glass windows embedded in the front walls of the great hall that men were still awake.

She hesitated for a moment, uncertain of what to do, but then decided to retire. Why should she alert these men to what she had seen? They would hardly believe her warnings anyway, not after she had so openly expressed her animosity toward them. She did not care to be further humiliated. Whatever will be, will be, whether one is prepared or not.

OSWALD THE SAILOR

———————— ■ ————————

"How many? Twenty?! Thirty!" Michael exclaimed as the English sailor showed by alternately closing and opening his fist how many adversaries he and his fellow crewmembers had fought against in Adaldalur Valley. This band of superior strength had nonetheless been chased off in a most valiant manner; the boy was sure of that, despite the fact that the man telling the story did not seem terribly threatening, emaciated as he was, with concave cheeks and foul-smelling bandages wrapped around his injured right arm. His name was Oswald Miller, and for the past five summers he had been sailing to Iceland.

"Better to be a fisherman off Iceland than forced into battle with those French mongrels," he told Michael in his native language, chuckling. "Though there's not much of a difference, since you Icelanders have become such godforsaken hooligans." The boy smiled and nodded, grasping barely half of what the man said, though his comprehension was growing by the day. The injured sailor did not have much other company available to him as most of the domestics ignored him, being fully aware of how he had received his injuries. A few of his countrymen from among the bishop's attendants had made brief visits to the hall in the first few days, before the other sailors returned to their ship, but few took the trouble to come after that. Not many of those men were of the same ilk as he, despite being from the same country.

Michael, however, sought out Oswald Miller's company, using every opportunity to talk to him in a strange mixture of Nordic and English, supplemented with various forms of hand-waving and gesturing.

The vessel *Bartholomew* sailed from King's Lynn, but Oswald had been born and raised in London and had travelled far and wide before beginning his voyages to Iceland. He had even fought for his heredetary king in France, and he'd escaped from great battles in Leirudalur Valley with only minor injuries. There the English had won a glorious victory after he himself had slain at least a dozen men.

"By then old Oswald considered himself to have done his duty in France and thought it best not tempt fate anymore in that godforsaken land," he said with a grin, revealing his decaying, gapped teeth, laugh lines appearing around his eyes. Michael involuntarily ran his tongue along his own teeth, all of which were whole, just as they were in everyone else he knew. Many of the English had black teeth. Might his own turn that color too, since he was half English?

"Anyway, a year later the wind turned," Oswald went on, spitting energetically into a spittoon on the floor through the holes in his teeth. "The goddamned French tortured nearly half our soldiers to death near Montargis. That was the same legion from which I'd been discharged after my heroic deeds."

"But the English are better now because they have sulphur from Iceland to make explosions and scare the living daylights out of the French," Michael said reverently in broken English.

The sailor shook his head with a grimace. "The sulphur is fine as far as it goes, but it hasn't helped us when it comes to the sorcery of the French. Black magic is the only thing that can explain the victory of that girl from Lorraine. They say it was proven when they finally captured her last year. And now she's said to be dead, burned at the stake like any other heretic and witch in the market square in Rouen last spring. That may turn the tables, though it is probably too late."

"A girl?" Michael stared at Oswald in disbelief, sure he had misheard. "A girl led the French army...and beat the English?!"

"Joan of Arc was a witch, pure and simple, and was in cahoots with the prince of darkness," Oswald reaffirmed with a frown. "A beastly she-devil she was, cavorting around the battlefield like a man with her hair cut short and astride a horse in full armor, spouting curses and spells so fierce that a black fog came over our men and they couldn't see a thing. Viciously slaughtered they were by those French bastards. God bless those valiant boys who fell at Orleans; may they rest in peace." He crossed himself with a pious expression, and Michael quickly followed suit, despite his doubts as to the validity of the story.

Then he had another thought and wrinkled his forehead. "Must all Englishmen fight wars for the king?"

Oswald nodded. "All except those who can be of other use, like sailing to Iceland, for example. The soldiers get stockfish as provisions and still more stockfish when they go to war. French livestock is not considered safe or dependable anymore." He chuckled softly, and his expression suggested that he was revisiting a few more memories. Then he grew serious. "Where did you say your father sailed from, boy?"

"His ship was from Bristol, but he left Iceland on another ship more than six months before I was born. He didn't even know about me."

"And no word from him since then?"

Michael shook his head dolefully. "Nothing." He added, so softly that it was almost inaudible: "My mother has had people ask about him at the Kolbeinsaros fishing station in the spring, when the ships come in from abroad. But these days they mostly come from King's Lynn and Hull."

"He may have given up the sea and probably has a family in Bristol," said Oswald pleasantly. "Men who have many mouths to feed also don't have to go to war. Or maybe he sailed to Greenland. Many men from Bristol do, and have done very well for themselves."

Michael brightened. "Really? My grandfather Thorsteinn has a ship that sails to Greenland, and land in the Eastern Settlement." Then he became downcast once more. "Thorsteinn would have ordered his men to kill my father if they heard of him being there."

"Well, if that had happened, you would have found out—right? And you haven't, so it's just as likely that he's alive and kicking," said Oswald reassuringly. He rearranged himself in bed, wincing in pain. "Run along now, boy, and fetch me something to quench this thirst. I'll recite an English poem for you. That'll make us both feel better."

Michael leapt to his feet. Herbal-Anna, who was sitting on a bed at the other end of the hall tending to one of her male patients, snorted loudly when he asked her for a drink of ale for Oswald. She ladled whey into a tin cup and handed it to him. "This is good enough for that louse. And does your mother know that you are always hanging around him and running his errands?"

Michael avoided her stern gaze and muttered something unintelligible before scampering away with the cup.

Oswald snorted as loudly as Anna had when he took a swig of the acidic drink. "What hideous ratsbane is this! Though it does get the job done," he said, wiping his mouth on his soiled sleeve. Then, in keeping with his word, he began to sing, his deep voice occasionally cracking on the highest notes. The verse was about a foolish carpenter from Canterbury who had a pretty wife and rented the garret of his house out to a clever young student who was well-versed in the secrets of love, as well as the stars:

The old carpenter, he found himself a wife,
And vowed to cherish her for all his life.
She was a lovely thing of just eighteen,
The prettiest girl that he had ever seen,
Yet distrust began to plague his aging heart;
From other folks he made her stay apart.
A foolish ploy; she was a dazzling swan,
And quick to be unfaithful to her man.
Oh this trap was entirely of his making.
It was his fault; there was no escaping.
The old adage he should have kept in mind,
That a woman of one's age is best to find,
For often there is strife twixt young and old,
And the end to wedlock easily foretold.

Just at that moment, Ragna entered the hall and stopped short when she heard the singing. A few elderly and derelict patients had raised themselves up in their beds, some looking foolish and baffled, not understanding a single word of the sailor's song and, indeed, looking like they had never heard a song before in their lives. Others were more sullen, offended by the ruckus that had roused them from their afternoon nap. Michael alone seemed contented and happy, sitting on a low stool by the sailor's bed and tapping his foot to the beat.

Oswald Miller's rough voice stopped singing in mid-verse. He had seen Ragna.

"Oh, beautiful, merciful lady, whose delicate hands saved my wretched life," he said, lowering his head with humility.

Ragna strode over to them with a furious expression, and Michael leapt to his feet. The smile vanished from his face and was replaced by obstinacy. She did not so much as waste a glance on the sailor.

"So here you are. Have you not heard anything of what I've been telling you?" she said angrily. "Why don't you listen? What do you think people will say about you loitering here in the company of this lout?"

"They can say what they want," he answered stubbornly, staring at her with flaming eyes. "Why should I care what others think when they don't even know me?"

Ragna was speechless. The boy was using words she herself had uttered a long time ago. She was saddened by the bitterness in his voice.

"People think ill of those who take up arms against ordained men, and so they should," she said, her voice slightly more kind.

"Oswald says the men from Grenjadarstadur ambushed them and none of them knew that there was a priest among them until Father Thorkell took off his helmet and showed his bare crown."

"Oh, is that what he says? And you believe him?!" She looked at her scowling son with mockery and astonishment, feeling a strange combination of love and repulsion. When had Michael gone from being a child to this adult-like boy, becoming almost as tall as her in the process? "Has he also told you how badly injured Thorkell and his men were after such an unwarranted attack, seeing that they were completely innocent?"

Michael nodded. "They were bleeding when they fled, him and two or three others. Father Thorkell was hit in the side with an iron arrow from a crossbow."

119

The color drained from Ragna's face, and she crossed herself. "Lord have mercy!" She glared at Oswald, who sent her a bewildered, gap-toothed smile, having understood nothing of the conversation other than that the mother was somewhat less kindly disposed toward him than the boy. "The English will get their just rewards, the almighty Lord will see to that," she said. "And now go, get to your chores, and don't let anyone see you in here again, fawning upon this man like a dog. I should have thought twice before I started attending to this rat."

Michael clenched his fist in impotent rage. "Why shouldn't I make friends with an English sailor in need? Or have you forgotten about my father?"

"You have but one father and that is God in heaven, and don't you dare answer back to me or so help me I will whip you!" she hissed furiously. Michael squeezed his mouth shut and strode to the door with his head held high. Opening it, he mumbled through clenched teeth, more for his own benefit than his mother's: "I do *so* have a father…and one day I'll find him."

A WALRUS-TOOTH COMB

The seal was easily recognized: a lily and sword in a cross on a shield, with a bird above. Her stepfather Thorsteinn's emblem. Ragna cracked the seal open and unfolded the vellum leaf with trembling hands; a croaking raven had flown before the bishop's postal delivery man as he rode up to the house. There were only a few lines, scribbled in Thorsteinn's hand: her mother was terminally ill on her deathbed. With the bishop's kind permission, Ragna should come to her immediately, and bring the boy with her. Urgent business awaited her.

She handed the letter to John Craxton, distraught. "My mother is ill."

He squinted his myopic eyes and slowly read the lawman's note, clearing his throat several times. "He does not say what ails her. I have recently had reports of an outbreak of pox on the West Fjords. This may mean that it has reached this part of the country."

"Whatever it is, I must go and see my mother," Ragna replied. "I received word from my sister Kristin a few weeks ago, after she had given birth to her first child, and she made no mention of an illness." She rubbed her damp palms together nervously. "If it is smallpox, then what is to be done? Surely there are many at risk of being infected and dying. Hundreds of people perished in the last epidemic a few decades ago."

"You're free to go as early as tomorrow. Keep calm and trust the Lord." The bishop placed a comforting hand on Ragna's shoulder, moving his fingers slowly and gently down her bare upper arm. His touch made her uncomfortable, and she flinched without knowing why.

"I will get someone to escort you. Stay as long as you need to," Craxton said kindly. "Your mother may well recover. Let us pray for God's mercy. But no one knows when it is their time. If indeed it is the pox, it is likely that others will be affected. The last time it passed through England, some formed blotches on the first day, while others spent days with fever and delirium before the pox broke out on their skins. They seemed more likely to survive than the others, and the older people did better than the young. The children were the first to die. He holds our life and death in His hands. The main thing is to help one another and trust that the righteous will receive God's mercy."

Before she and Michael rode away the following morning, the bishop gave Ragna a large, closed pail filled with consecrated water from the cathedral's baptism font. It was the most potent—and, indeed, the only—medicine against the evil pestilence.

◇❖◇

Sigridur was dying. But it wasn't the pox.

She pulled back the duvet and unbuttoned the neckline of her thin linen caftan to reveal her swollen, red-blue breasts to her daughter. The skin was scabrous and slightly indented above the left nipple. An ugly, festering sore had eaten through her skin to the flesh. "Look. It's horribly painful. It started here first, in early spring, hard and sore. It then moved into the pit of my arm and now it is all over my insides. The pain is so great that I can hardly get out of bed. The priest calls it the canker malady. It won't be long until it has me completely consumed. That's if I don't give up the ghost first from the coughing. Hopefully I will find peace and get my eternal rest before Michaelmas. I can no longer keep down any proper nourishment." She smiled in spite of this death sentence, courageous and calm, yet visibly emaciated from her hopeless battle against the chronic pain. Her matted eyes had dark circles beneath them; her skin, taut over the bones of her face, had the yellowish veneer of death. There was visible swelling beneath her jawline. Scraggly strands of hair that once had cascaded down in auburn waves peeked from beneath her nightcap, hoary and lifeless.

Sigridur took Ragna's hands and held them in her own, stroking her hot, dry fingers over them. The veins on her hands stood out, and her nails were convex and speckled with white. "It's good to have you here, Ragna my dearest. There's so much I want to say to you while I still have time."

Ragna searched for a response but found none. She had a big lump in her throat that refused to leave, no matter how often she swallowed. The corners of her eyes stung. How could her mother be dying? Surely it wasn't true. Surely something could be done.

"How would the priest know what this affliction is and whether or not it can be cured?" she finally asked in a choked voice, almost angrily. "Father Pall knows nothing about healing. What would he know about it? Has he tried bloodletting to help you?"

"It wasn't Pall who said it," said Sigridur, somewhat awkwardly. She lowered her voice, taking on a slight warning tone. "It was Father Thorkell Gudbjartsson, who recently arrived from Grenjadarstadur to discuss some matter concerning the bishop with your foster-father. He is well informed about various illnesses and has even transcribed all sorts of pertinent knowledge from foreign books. Information on how to make balms and extracts, for example. He claims bloodletting will do little good at this stage. He has given me this concoction, and it has relieved the pain a little and helps me to rest." She produced a small, round, glass flask containing a murky brownish liquid and showed it to Ragna, then took a gulp, grimaced, and sighed. "It's strong, and salty, too, but it seems to help. It's made from some kind of powder from foreign plants, ground up with nigella seeds and liquor."

It took Ragna a moment to comprehend her mother's words. She sat next to her on the bed and tried to collect her thoughts. Anger, happiness, sadness, surprise—all swirled inside her and she could not tell them apart. Her mother was dying and about to leave her orphaned and alone in the world; Thorkell was healed from his wounds and currently here at Akrar, seeking the support of her people against the English. She looked at Sigridur, who was leaning backward against the feather pillows, her eyes closed, evidently exhausted. How much did she know? Had she heard about the battle in Adaldalur? Surely Thorsteinn would have spared her news that might cause her anxiety and agitation; after all, she had enough on her mind. Moreover, he had always been a reticent man and self-directed in most things, not feeling a need to consult with his wife, even though all of his possessions were hers, and hers his. He was not likely to ask her advice on matters of business or politics at this time, any more than he had in the past.

"Gudbjartur and his son Thorkell wanted Thorleiksstadur, which I inherited from my parents, but Thorsteinn refused." Sigridur spoke without opening her eyes, almost as if she had read her daughter's mind. "He felt you had brought such shame upon us that you had lost your claim to that fine property. And I was so gutless that I let him decide," she said softly. Ragna said nothing, just stared straight ahead, her silence fraught with accusation.

Sigridur opened her eyes and looked at her daughter, sad and desolate. "A woman must surrender to her husband and strive to please him, according to the apostle Paul."

"That's what they say." Abrupt agreement, full of bitterness. No hint of forgiveness in her voice. How different things might have been if her mother had had the courage to side with her daughter instead of Thorsteinn. Was it not a mother's duty to put love for her child, her own flesh and blood, before everything else—even her desire to please her husband? And yet it was rarely so. Still, why cry about things that couldn't be changed, especially at a time like this? Ragna felt ashamed of having such ugly thoughts at her mother's deathbed. After all, the list of her own sins was already more than full.

The silence between them was becoming oppressive.

Finally, in a weak voice, Sigridur asked about her grandson. "How does my sweet Michael like Holar, Ragna?"

Ragna had left Michael at a nearby farm, despite his protestations. The bishop's remark that children were the first to die from the pox had alarmed her. But she did not mention that reason to her mother, only said that he'd wanted to see his friend at Grund after a lengthy absence. The Akrar residents apparently had not heard about the outbreak of pox on the West Fjords, and at this stage it was just as well that her mother not find out.

"The clerics say he has a good aptitude for learning and is bright, but they feel that he has a bit of a wild temper." Ragna ran her thumb along her chin as she often did when deep in thought. "I have heard the other schoolboys call him a Skraeling, and they exclude him from their games," she added brusquely. "It upsets him, though he does not speak to me about it."

"Have you told him the story of the seal woman?" Sigridur asked and raised herself up in bed with difficulty, gasping with pain at every movement.

Ragna arranged her mother's pillows and pulled the duvet over her. "I can hardly remember that story well enough to tell it," she said. "It's been so long since grandmother told it to me. I was only a wee girl then, and she recited so many strange tales and sang such odd songs."

"Your father's people have passed the story of the seal woman down through the generations for more than a century. It must not be forgotten," Sigridur said in a warning tone. "We must respect our family stories and pass them on so that they are not lost."

"Tell me now," said Ragna gently, relieved that their conversation had taken a different turn. "Tell me about the seal woman, and I shall tell Michael and later his children."

"You sound just as you did when you were small and wanted your way. You always thought you'd better be able to get it if you spoke gently." Her mother smiled a wistful smile that vanished almost as quickly as it appeared. "Do you remember when we left Hvalsey? Remember how long you pleaded with us after we sailed from the coast to go back and leave you there?"

Ragna nodded. "I did not want to leave grandmother or my cousins, and I was afraid to sail out onto the sea. It seemed so vast and endless."

"The people of the Eastern Settlement are good people, Ragna," her mother said firmly. "And though the Lord took all your siblings that were born there, the time in Greenland was a blessing. It saved us. The plague that claimed all my people here

at home did not reach Greenland. It is a harsh land but also bountiful, and its people are better protected against many calamities
than the people here, whether from plagues or natural disasters
or violence at the hands of foreign plunderers..."

Sigridur was silent and stared straight ahead, her eyes distant. Then in a hypnotic voice she began to tell the tale of the seal
woman. She was a good storyteller, and images of precipitous,
snow-covered mountains and icebergs in a long fjord, floating in
an ice-blue sea, sprung to life in Ragna's mind. They were vague
at first, but then the mists of time gradually lifted and behind her
eyelids she could see the sun dancing on sea and firn, and the
summer sky above Greenland, bluer than all things blue.

"There were few women in the Eastern Settlement in those
days, too few for all men of marrying age to be able to take a wife,
and on many farms the women died young from their brood of
children, as often happens. Your great-grandfather was past middle age and unmarried when this story happened; he was a bit of
a loner and liked to hunt on his own, not with the other settlers
in Hvalseyjarfjord. He was a good, generous man, who shared
his catch—seals, fish, and birds—with his neighbors. One night
in spring, while he was travelling far from home, searching for
seals in a remote cove, he saw a group of young women on the
shore, dancing a strange dance and singing songs in no-man's
language." And Sigridur began to sing a strange, incomprehensible song, disjointed tones that sounded almost like the warbling
of birds. Ragna smiled as she recognized it; it had been sung to
her as a child, and she had sung it to Michael when he was small.
And once to his father.

"There were seven women, exquisitely beautiful, their movements graceful and their bodies taut and shimmering, and a short
distance away, on a large boulder, were seven sealskins. The man

became mad with desire and crept closer, seized one of the seal-skins, and hid it. Then he hid behind the boulder and watched the women, mesmerized. When they stopped dancing, they put on their skins and dove into the sea—all but one, who could not find hers. She shouted and wept, and soon he appeared from behind the boulder to comfort her. He asked her to become his wife and promised that she would have her skin back in seven years' time. The seal woman was drawn to the man, for he was kind and had a good physique. She accepted his proposal. Eventually she gave birth to a daughter who was dark-skinned and had a broad face just like hers, high cheekbones, black hair, and the eyes of a seal. The seal woman doted on the infant girl; she sang to her for hours and told her stories about the sea mother at the bottom of the ocean and all the creatures that live there: fishes and seals and whales and polar bears, mermaids and mermen. But when seven years had passed, the man could not bear to keep his promise, for he loved the woman and did not want their daughter to grow up motherless. The seal woman cried bitterly and said she had to go home, otherwise she would wither and die, but the man would not give in." Sigridur paused and coughed with loud, hacking sounds. She cleared her throat, then continued, her voice hoarse: "The daughter could not endure her mother's cries of grief. So one night she looked all through the house until she found the sealskin where her father had hidden it in the attic. She gave it to her mother. With salty tears the seal woman bid farewell to her daughter on the shore, donned her skin, and dove into the sea. She was never seen in the guise of a human again. Your great-grandfather grieved desperately for her. Yet during his hunts he fared better than ever before, and their descendants have never suffered scarcity, even when times have been rough in Greenland and others have starved. The grass in the fields belonging to your father's people has always been more verdant than in other fields, and cod bite on all of their hooks, even when the next fjord is empty of fish. Most of your great-grandmother's descendants have had that same facial appearance that people here find dark and ugly. But in Hvalseyjarfjord, people know the truth, and they consider it auspicious to have the same countenance as the seal woman. You must tell Michael this and teach him to be proud of who he is, different from the rest. Unique."

Sigridur whispered the last words with anguish. Clearly the pain was engulfing her once more and she could barely stifle her moans. She reached for the medicine flask and took a swig of the infusion.

"Go now, dearest Ragna. Go and leave me be," she said in a tormented voice, waving a hand at her daughter. "I must rest."

Ragna remained sitting on the bed. She did not want to go into the great hall and have to face Thorkell—not yet. She needed time to think, and anyway, she felt she should stay by her mother's side now, when there was no escaping the pain. And yet, she was afraid.

"Wouldn't you like me to stay a while longer?" she said and put her hand around Sigridur's clenched fist. Her mother's palms had deep red marks where the fingernails had dug in. "Let me sing for you, dearest Mamma..."

Softly she began to sing, the same incomprehensible words that her mother had sung before: "*Qa-vam-mut kak-kak qii-ma-naq qa-vam-mut...*"

Sigridur's eyes were shrouded in pain. She turned away, tormented, and howled into her pillow, stuffing a corner into her mouth to stifle the sound. Ragna kept singing, filled with dread at her mother's howling, wanting above all else to run away. Almost inadvertently she removed her shoes and slipped into bed with her mother, placing her body in a spoon position with her arm across the older woman, warming her whole body with hers. Perhaps Sigridur had not had the resolve to stand by her daughter the way mothers should, even when they risk their husband's disapproval, yet Ragna owed her her life. The very least she could do to thank her mother was to ease her death throes, even if just a little.

Much later, Sigridur's howls of pain subsided and they both fell into a slumber, the older woman first. Ragna listened to her ragged breathing deepen and thought about this woman who had become a stranger to her, a woman that she had nonetheless known longer than anyone else. But then, who can ever truly know their own mother?

In the shadows, over by the wall, the angel of death awaited.

⬦

Ragna was roused by voices near the door. She did not know how long she had slept. It felt to her like only a short while, but she could see that the tallow candle in the wall candle holder had nearly burned down. She heard her foster-father's voice, and then Thorsteinn entered the room. She placed a finger on her lips to silence him, but to no avail: her mother was already awake. Quickly she brushed the strands of hair away from her face and greeted her husband. He kissed her, then kissed Ragna on both cheeks. His thick beard was soft to the touch. Thorsteinn was a few winters older than his wife, and his reddish complexion exuded energy even though his dark hair and beard were streaked with silver. Sigridur's pallid face appeared even more ghostlike to Ragna, now that she saw them next to each other.

Thorsteinn sat down in a chair opposite the bed, crossed his arms, and looked at them inquisitively.

"So, Ragna, how do you feel about the move to Greenland?"

She was startled. "Move to Greenland?" she asked, surprised. "What do you mean?"

"We have not discussed the letter, Thorsteinn," Sigridur said feebly. "I couldn't; it was too soon."

"What letter?" Ragna asked warily. "From whom?"

"The *Christopher* of Hull arrived from Greenland a week ago," Thorsteinn answered. "With the ship came a letter from your people in Hvalseyjarfjord—your aunt Thorhildur and her husband Sigurdur. They have managed our holdings there since we left for Iceland."

"*Your* holdings, Ragna," Sigridur corrected him with an apologetic glance. "Hvalsey will be yours when I have passed, with all its assets and properties."

"The land belongs to all of us, though it is yours by virtue of inheritance, as you are Gauti's only surviving child," said Thorsteinn drily. "Let us not forget that it is I who has made sure that tithes were collected, and I have acted as intermediary in the stockfish trade for the farmers in the fjord. Indeed, I have overseen the interests of all the Eastern Settlement throughout the years, to the great advantage of our family and everyone there." He paused before continuing. "The old couple has not been capable of much in recent years. They're getting on, and only one of their ten children has lived at one time. Now their only daughter—indeed their only child who survived to adulthood—has passed, leaving a husband and three promising sons. Her husband, Valur Hauksson, has overseen the property and the stockfish trade in Hvalseyjarfjord. He is a hardworking, capable man, even if he is from the Western Settlement."

"And how does this letter concern me?" asked Ragna.

"Valur seeks your hand in marriage, and after careful consideration, your mother and I have decided that he shall have it."

Ragna was speechless. She stared at Thorsteinn and then her mother, filled with disbelief. "You have made such a decision without consulting me?" She stood up from the bed with as much dignity as she could muster and placed her hands on her hips, tilting her head back. "I am no longer a child who can be forced into submission and ordered around at will!"

"Ragna my dearest, please, we only want what is best for you," Sigridur said miserably and reached for her hand. "Hear your foster-father out. There are many arguments in favor of this proposal. You should be grateful that he has arranged it."

"The Bible states that thou shalt honor your father and your mother," Thorsteinn said curtly, standing up to face Ragna. They were about the same height. "Again, he is a hardworking man, and it would be to our great advantage to have him as a son-in-law. We need good men in Hvalsey, and this is the best way to secure our connections with the Eastern Settlement. This is highly important now that the English have started to show an added interest in the fish trade there and are looking to trade with the Greenlanders directly. Obviously a man who owns a share of the land and earns revenues from it is far more trustworthy than any ordinary administrator. He has a vested interest in the proper management of his own land."

She wanted most of all to scream, but when she opened her mouth, her voice was barely audible. "And what do I stand to gain from this arrangement?"

"Ragna, you are well past the common age for marriage," Thorsteinn said gently. "You are perfectly aware of why suitors have not appeared. You could lose your life in giving birth to another child, and the sin that is at the root of that affliction is known to all in these parts. Valur already has three sons, who are all likely to live. They are also related to you by blood—and they need a mother. The situation could not be more favorable."

"Valur understands how things stand with Michael and has offered to adopt him as his own son," said Sigridur. "He will then have the same right to inheritance as Valur's own sons. For his sake as well as your own, you should be happy about this arrangement, my dear."

Ragna let her arms drop down by her sides. She sat down on the edge of the bed, downcast and wan. "But what about his education at Holar? He might be able to become a deacon, or even a priest," she said glumly. She felt dejected. Was there no way out of this?

"How can you entertain such thoughts, Ragna? You know that a bastard cannot be ordained," Thorsteinn replied, evidently surprised. He added, more kindly: "The boy would make a good seaman and would no doubt welcome the opportunity to sail. He might even grow up to become first mate. Moreover, if he is adopted, he could be ordained in Greenland, should that be his wish."

Ragna glanced sideways at her mother, but Sigridur avoided her daughter's eyes. She looked despondent. Thoughts whirled through Ragna's head. Could they force her to go? Michael could become a legal heir. She would probably never see Thorkell, or Iceland, again. She would be mistress of her own farm, respected by all in the district. What would her life be like if she refused? Would the bishop keep her on as housekeeper, against her parents' will? Not likely. And what if she went to live with Thorkell at Grenjadarstadur, became his mistress in plain view of all— he with his three illegitimate children, and perhaps even more?

Everyone would look on her with contempt, she was sure of that. Could she bring herself to oppose her mother on her deathbed, to cause her more grief?

"What is the age of this man?" she asked after a brief silence.

Thorsteinn smiled. "Just like a woman to think of such things first," he said, pleased. "Valur is just thirty, a very good age. The two elder sons are of a similar age to Michael, and the youngest is five or six winters old. The poor things have been motherless for the last two years."

"How did the mother die?"

Sigridur and Thorsteinn looked at one another uncertainly, like each wanted the other to answer. Ragna guessed the answer. "In childbirth?" They both nodded.

"The child was so large that it had to be cut out of the poor woman," said Sigridur, her voice hoarse. "The blood loss killed her." All three were silent, thinking back to Michael's devastating birth, twelve years earlier. The only sound was Sigridur's wheezing breath, like something was seething inside her.

Ragna summoned her courage. "Would we sail next spring?"

The lawman shook his head. "Klaengur will sail the *Christopher* back to Greenland on Michaelmas at the latest, in ten days' time. He'll spend the winter in Gardar. There is a dire shortage of goods in the Eastern Settlement, and we must help the people in their time of need. They don't even have flour to make altar bread and have started using seaweed for baking. In return we shall receive ample payment in stockfish that will be sent to England in the spring, when fish stocks are low after Lent and the price as high as it can be."

"Michaelmas!" Ragna exclaimed.

"Your mother will be immensely relieved to know that your future is secure before she passes," Thorsteinn said firmly and looked at his wife, who nodded.

"But is my future not secure at Holar? Bishop Craxton says he is much pleased with my work," said Ragna willfully, resisting the sway that death held over life. "As the bishop's housekeeper, I am respected."

Thorsteinn's countenance grew dim. "The people's respect for the bishop is declining rapidly, Ragna, as is his influence—that is, if things continue along this path. He has given protection to English ribalds who have ridden through the districts marauding and injuring, and even killing people. Soon he will have to pay for his poor judgment. Things will come to a head, sooner rather than later."

Sigridur took her daughter's arm, gently. "These are turbulent times, Ragna. You would be safer in Greenland, a married woman on your own land, that you inherited from your father." She looked at Thorsteinn. "Fetch the gift that Valur sent her, dear. It is in my chest."

The lawman lifted the lid of a large oak chest at the foot of the bed and glanced through its contents, then removed a small package that had been tied with a leather string. He handed it to Ragna. She unraveled the string and took out a hair comb from a sheath of speckled gray sealskin. The comb was skillfully carved from a milky white walrus tooth, and on it was her name, engraved in runic letters: *I belong to Ragna*. The inscription was encircled with dragon tails, a tiny dragon head carved at each end.

"He is skilled with his hands, like all his kin. They are all accomplished craftsmen," said Thorsteinn. Ragna weighed the comb in her hand, its teeth sharp, the surface of the comb polished to a silky finish. She ran it through the thick tresses that cascaded loosely around her shoulders.

"It is beautiful, is it not?" Sigridur said. Ragna reluctantly concurred. Yes, it was beautiful. Surely only a good man could transform the tooth of an animal into an object of such beauty. Was there any point in resisting? Parents make the rules; daughters obey. That was the way of the world.

She wondered what Thorkell would say.

◈

The air was acrid from the smoke coming from the large fireplace, yet the great hall was not warm. Rather than wafting out through the small porthole in the roof above the fire, the smoke swirled forward into the hall, while the chill of autumn slipped in through the opening. The wind had picked up from the north as the afternoon wore on. Servants added brushwood to the fire, their eyes watering and faces dark with soot.

Many people had gathered for dinner. Kristin Thorsteinsdottir had come from Holl on Hofdastrond to see her mother, probably for the last time. She had her swaddled firstborn Ingvaldur with her, and she was accompanied by all her in-laws. The heaviness in Sigridur's chest had increased, her breathing was crackly, and it was clear that her days on this earth would soon come to an end. Kristin, who had barely known illness in all of her nineteen winters, was repulsed by sickness and suffering. Consequently, she had been keeping her distance, and anyway, she had a newborn to look after.

Michael sat on the women's bench, on Kristin's left. He could barely keep his eyes off the cheerful infant in her lap, amazed that something so small and delicate could actually breathe and exist in the world. No less astonishing was the fact that his aunt Kristin, who was only a few winters his senior, was now a mother, having given birth to this chubby little imp. Ragna sat on her sister's right and listened indifferently to her descriptions of the suffering she'd endured during the birth, relayed in such detail that Michael alternately blushed and went pale, counting his blessings to be of the male gender. A notch above, at the high table, sat Thorsteinn the lawman with his son-in-law Helgi to one side, along with his parents, Gudni and Thorbjorg of Holl. On Thorsteinn's other side was Bjorn Eyjolfsson, the king's magistrate, and next to him Hallur of Thorleiksstadir, Thorsteinn's brother, and Father Thorkell Gudbjartsson of Grenjadarstadur.

Ragna and Thorkell had not yet spoken, and he paid her no particular attention, appearing deep in conversation with his fellow diners. This aroused Ragna's interest a great deal more than Kristin's account of her painful childbirth. From what she could discern, it sounded like sailors from the balinger *Bartholomew* had continued their marauding through the nearby districts. Thorkell had been injured in the side but not badly, thanks be to God and the mail shirt that he had borrowed. It had happened after he and his band of men had set off in pursuit of the villains. They had received word that the English were raiding farms in Reykjahverfi district, stealing fish and livestock.

Bjorn the magistrate, a slightly stooped man with a long face and red nose, groaned and grunted and repeatedly affirmed that he would have done the very same thing if he had known. Unfortunately, he had been off in Eyjafjord on business along with both of his prosecutors, since an infamous horse trader north of Sletta had been found guilty of stealing sheep and horses and had subsequently been sentenced to death by hanging.

"Those villains stole four hundred fish, three holds of stock-fish, and seven horses. The women were home all alone with no idea of those offenses being committed under the cloak of dark-ness," he said and shook his head in consternation, his shoulders drooping even further. "Mongrels."

"If we don't gather our forces soon to bring these men to jus-tice, we can expect them to reach the Reynistadur abbey before too long," said Thorkell. His voice was impassioned, and there was fire in his eyes. "Those English dogs have proven that they hold nothing sacred and care nothing for law and order. Seven years hence, mobs from King's Lynn and York laid Olafsfjardarherad district and Hrisey Island to waste. They stripped Grimsey church of all its treasures, including chalices and clocks, and burned the Husavik church to the ground. And what came from those charges we sent to the king? Nothing, I tell you! None of the villains were apprehended." He leaned forward, passionate and intense; the room had grown silent, and all eyes were on him. "And now, again, we have gangs marauding through the district. Let us not think for a moment that we shall have help from Norway, especially since most of the fleet in Bergen harbor has been burned by pirates. In the south the English have taken both the Westman Islands and Hafnarfjord, and ended all fish-ing from local stations by demolishing boats and maiming, even killing, fishermen. And now we have reports of children and adolescents being sold into slavery to England, even though a handful of perpetrators were sentenced there last year. They take both our fish and our children. How can we live with any sort of dignity when such deeds go unpunished? Are we not men to put an end to these assaults?!"

He looked sharply over the benches and met the severe looks of men and women at each glance. The people were outraged along with him. Yes, the English had most certainly gone too far. It was high time for it to end. The lawman raised his silver-trimmed drinking horn and proposed a toast, that those who now plagued the country with violence would be caught and punished. In that instant the servant women entered the hall with food, placing grilled legs of lamb on large serving plates made of tin on the tables. The scent of the piping hot meat was delectable, and the guests could think of little else. And so the feast began, with toasts being drunk to the cook and to holy men, the Mother of God and the Holy Trinity up above, not forgetting Sigridur, mistress of the house, who lay in her quarters in a virtual coma while her kinsmen and other guests enjoyed their meal.

Ragna could not eat much; she only nibbled on the bread that was served with the lamb. The fat slab of meat on her plate remained untouched. Her mother owned dozens of shallow wooden plates, turned in England, that had beautifully carved patterns along their edges. She drank all the toasts, and soon the ale went to her head and her face became flushed. The ale was made from English malt, the red wine purchased from English traders. Occasionally she thought that Thorkell had glanced at her quickly, but when she looked up, he was looking the other way. Everything was moving so fast. How could she keep track when so much was happening at once? There was too much chaos.

Klaengur the captain stood up and began reciting a verse about Skidi:

Tallest of men, thin as a reed,
Long arms at his side,
Walking hunched like one aggrieved,
With hands both big and wide,
Crooked teeth and scraggly beard,

His facial bones protrude,
Insolent and sometimes feared,
To noblemen is crude.

The guests laughed, and the atmosphere in the hall changed. The rage that had coursed through the guests' veins in the wake of Thorkell's speech gave way to cheer. All giggled at the tale of the wandering wretch Skidi, who had travelled all the way from the western districts, south across Norway and over to Denmark, to Asgard, to visit with Odinn. There he was invited to sit next to this most revered of the Norse gods in Valhalla:

Odinn asked him at that point,
Seeking his advice:
"Are there many more than you,
In the land of ice?"

❖

I look at these people all around me. My people. They laugh and talk and argue and cry and mourn. They love and hate. Or do they? My sister coddles her son, so fair and lovely, healthy and promising; no doubt he will be the first of many, conceived in holy wedlock. What is bound together on earth is likewise so in heaven. He shall inherit this land. The future is his. The English bastard, my son, healthy and promising, with his dark eyes and dark complexion, also smiles at the little boy, but in his eyes there is bitterness because he knows how it has all been arranged. His future is uncertain. Thorsteinn, my foster-father, has unexpressed anguish in his eyes because my mother is dying. She is leaving him, having taken her last rites and received the final anointing, and is waiting for death to come. He suffers, just like poor Gudridur Aladottir when everything had been taken from her, even though he holds greater earthly possessions than most other people in these districts.

Thorkell, my lover and a servant of God, is out for revenge. He seeks to punish those who induce hatred in his heart. And he wants power, in this world and the next, on both sides of the grave. Knowledge is the only way to gain real power—did he not tell me that once? Will he ever have enough to be satisfied?

And who am I, Ragna Gautadottir? A fallen woman, who mourns for the life she never lived, the life that stretches out before her, and the people she has left behind.

How do you break the bond between two hearts?

◈

The applause and shouting of the guests as Klaengur finished his verse brought her to her senses. *It is almost like people are at a wedding banquet,* she thought, and there was a stinging in her heart. *Does no one remember my mother, who lies on her death-bed in her quarters?* She stood up abruptly, spilling her drinking horn. Wine splashed onto her lap. A burgundy stain appeared on her white linen apron, widening and expanding, almost like blood. She quickly untied her apron, embarrassed, but none of the guests had noticed, save for Thorkell, who watched her with a grave expression. She pretended not to see him and hastened out of the hall, along the corridor, and into the sleeping quarters.

Sigridur's wide-open, blue-gray eyes seemed to stare into an endless distance. Her pupils were dilated, and she wore a frightened expression. There was no sign of ethereal tranquility and peace in her countenance. Her mouth hung open, and rivulets of blood-laced saliva ran down her chin and onto her chest. Her hands were clenched, clutching a rosary against her chest. On the floor lay the glass flask from Thorkell, shattered, in a puddle of brown liquid. Ragna stood motionless for a long time, rigid as the body in front of her. Then she leaned over and closed her mother's eyelids with her thumbs. She placed her palm under her jaw, pushing it upward. The chin was still warm and sank down again as soon as she released it. It would have to be tied with a cloth. She crossed her mother's arms over her chest, leaving the rosary between her fingers.

Ragna sat down on the edge of the bed and put her face in her hands. She began to sob uncontrollably, in spurts, like a glacial river ridding itself of ice. Wailing, she rocked back and forth; it was so painful, so unbelievably painful, to be an orphan. So alone, so horribly alone...

The door opened and Thorkell stepped in, closing the door gently behind him. She looked up at him, her eyes swollen and red.

"She died alone, Thorkell! She gasped for breath, her last breath, while we ate and drank and made toasts and sang and laughed. May the Lord forgive us for leaving her so alone!"

He walked to the bed and put a finger on Sigridur's swollen jugular vein, but found no pulse. He made the sign of the cross over her.

"She has found rest and peace. She has been released from the torment of this worldly existence, dearest Ragna. She's with God's angels in paradise now, with your brothers and sisters, who have waited so long to see their mother." He bent down on one knee in front of her, took her head in both hands, and wiped the tears out of the corners of her eyes with his thumbs, gently and lovingly. "Don't cry, my love, I am here," he whispered. "I'm here with you."

They looked into each other's eyes, and she saw his tenderness give way to that strange smoldering look that always made her uneasy. He covered her face with kisses, his cool lips on her cheeks, forehead, temples, lips. Probing kisses full of desire and roughness; kisses that demanded reciprocation. "God, how I have missed you this summer!" he said, short of breath, preventing her from answering by kissing her mouth. His tongue slipped in through her lips and played with hers, and she tasted the liquor on his breath. His hands cupped her breasts, and the tips of his fingers caressed her nipples until they grew hard. His caresses set off a flame in her belly that was entirely inappropriate in front of her dead mother. Ragna pushed him away, more roughly than she had intended. "Thorkell, stop it! Have you drank away all your good sense?!"

He fell backwards, upset. "I'm sorry, dearest. I lose all control in your presence. I didn't mean to…please forgive me, wretched sinner that I am." His deep-blue eyes were moist and glistening, and he looked so miserable that she didn't have the heart to be angry with him.

"I have also missed you," she admitted softly.

"Then come to Grenjadarstadur with me. You know you belong there," he said tenderly. He stroked her tear-stained cheeks, swept a lock of hair away from her face, and placed it behind her ear. "You belong by my side, Ragna. I need you with me."

She was going to answer and tell him not to speak of this again because she no longer had a choice, if she had ever had one. But at that moment Thorsteinn entered the sleeping quarters, followed by Kristin, holding her son. Thorkell leapt to his feet, nearly falling over in haste. They did not ask why he had been kneeling on the floor, only registered the fact that Sigridur's hacking breath was no longer audible, her eyes were shut, and her hands crossed over her chest.

"Were you with her when she passed?" Thorsteinn asked hoarsely, addressing Ragna. He reeled slightly and held on to the bedpost for support. Wretchedly she shook her head and sniffled.

"I left her before dinner. She was feeling all right then and was going to try to sleep. Then when I came to check on her a little while ago…" She swallowed and was unable to speak further.

Thorsteinn stood silent and motionless, gazing at the body of his wife, his eyes dry and his face devoid of expression. His jaw flexed when he gritted his teeth, and his eyes narrowed slightly, like he was trying to hold back moisture. It had been twenty-three years since their marriage in Hvalsey. None of her close relatives had been alive to give her away, all of them dead from the plague, and she herself a widow. She gave herself to him, in her own church. Not much persuasion was needed; he came from a family that was as wealthy as hers, though his holdings were not quite as extensive. And with him she returned to Iceland, leaving behind the churchyard that held five of the six children she had borne in Greenland, along with the man who had been chosen for her by her parents when she was still a child. She left the grief and the biting winter frost behind, and the ominous draft that had a way of slipping into children's lungs even when they were swaddled in woolen blankets and seal and polar bear pelts laid under them in the crib. She had given him a daughter and a son, stillborn. The boy would have been an idiot had he lived, his tiny face round like a full moon and his dark-blue eyes more slanted than those of a Greenlandic Skraeling, and moreover with a harelip. He was buried to the north of the churchyard, outside its walls, according to custom. And she had painstakingly tended to his resting place, more than any other, every summer; she had brought flowers from far and wide and made his a colorful grave, much larger than the coffin that had been put together around him. And now she, too, was gone. The breath had abandoned the tortured flesh, and with it her life, leaving behind a cold and rigid corpse. How swiftly it had happened. She who had never been unwell until last summer, who had never complained of any illness before then.

Little Ingvaldur, the legitimate and longed-for heir, broke the silence with his crying. He was a robust boy who needed to drink often—so often, in fact, that his mother had hired a young, healthy wet nurse to better be able to nourish him.

"She was a good and gentle woman," Thorsteinn said and turned, leaving the room quickly. Thorkell followed him.

The sisters began to wash their mother's body.

A BED-CURTAIN MADE OF VELVET

Nearly all the residents of Blonduhlid came out for the funeral, as did the people from Vidvik district and beyond. The church at Akrar was filled to the rafters, so many had to stand outside. Some people remarked that it might have been better to hold the funeral service for such a good, well-liked woman at Holar cathedral. But such an idea was quickly dismissed. For one thing, Sigridur's parents, Bjorn the Rich Brynjolfsson and Malfridur Eiriksdottir, and her siblings, Malmfridur and Olafur, had all been buried beneath the floor of Akrar church. Sigridur would have wanted to rest with her kin. Furthermore, it was being said that warmth between the lawman and the bishop was at an unprecedented low, after the latter had offered sanctuary to English lawbreakers.

Michael should have been in the front row with Thorsteinn, the father and son from Holl, and other men close to the deceased. Instead, he had been elbowed by the crowd towards the southern wall of the church. He stood pinned between Bjorn the magistrate and a lumbering, frocked monk whose face was concealed by a hood. He had arrived late at the church and so had only himself to blame that he wasn't able to be at the grave that had been opened in the stone floor. Yet he was near enough to smell the scent of moist earth. His mother was at the north end of the church with the other women; she and Kristin were probably sitting on his grandmother's pew. Surely Thorsteinn would not notice Michael's absence. He had barely spoken to anyone since Sigridur passed, and he appeared to have aged many years during those three days that had passed since the body had been laid out.

The boy had felt strange on the inside when he kissed his dead grandmother. There was like an empty coldness in his chest where previously there had been a warm feeling toward her. At first he had been happy to come to Akrar after a year away. He had even been tempted to ask whether he could be spared from returning to Holar, where he was at the mercy of the schoolboys and expected only scorn and ridicule. But upon seeing his grandmother's body, the feeling vanished and he was overcome with feelings of terrible loneliness and heartache. There was no longer anyone who cared for him at Akrar, so it was no longer his home. No matter that Kristin and Helgi would soon move from Hofdastrond and take up residence there. His aunt was now a grown woman, married, and had a child of her own. Previously they had been like siblings, but were now like strangers. They had often laughed and joked with each other, but now they moved quietly and listlessly through the halls and rooms.

Consequently, his mother's announcement about her proposed marriage and their imminent move to Greenland came like a deliverance. Michael could not stop himself from smiling, in spite of being at his grandmother's funeral. He thought of all the new and exciting things that lay ahead: crossing the ocean on a ship, a new country, new family, new life, him being adopted and allowed to inherit from his mother and foster-father. No one would call him a bastard again. The boy clenched his fist and punched it firmly into the palm of his other hand, as though demonstrating what he would do to the person who dared utter such an indignity. His grin grew even wider when he remembered what Oswald Miller had said about seamen from Bristol sailing to Greenland more than any other country. Maybe Michael, crewmember of the *Trinity* of Bristol, would turn up in Hvalseyjarfjord next summer! That way he wouldn't have to go looking for him when he got older, like he had planned to. And even if he did, at least he would have secured himself a place on a ship and would be able to explore the world on his own.

"What's with the wide grin, boy, in the middle of the service?"

Michael jumped and instantly rearranged his expression into something more befitting to the occasion. Bjorn the magistrate shook his head sternly and pushed Michael forward to where there was a bit more space. He then continued his discussion with the portly monk at his side in a quiet voice. Inside the choir, old Father Pall intoned the gospel. Michael began to pay attention to the exchange of the two men behind him; after all, it was hard to miss what they were saying.

"How many men do you have?" asked the magistrate quietly.

"We are thirty in all, but the ordained individual does not intend to carry weapons, apart from the holy cross, regardless of the bishop's excommunication," whispered the monk. Michael was instantly curious. He stood perfectly still, listening for the magistrate's reply.

"I'll have as many as that by the time the men from Thingeyjarsysla district arrive."

The monk sniffed. "Does that include the good Father Thorkell? He will hardly settle for holding a cross. He never has."

"Thorkell has rallied the men and secured their allegiance, even that of the lawman, Thorsteinn, and the men of Holl. Say what you will about him, he has managed to turn their hearts and minds against the English," Bjorn answered.

The monk chortled. Michael found this strange. It was like the magistrate had said something funny. "No doubt Craxton is having major regrets about giving Grenjadarstadur to him. Thorkell has caused him more trouble than I ever could have, even if I'd not been driven away."

At that moment the boy realized who was hiding beneath the monk's hood, though he did not have the nerve to turn around to confirm it. It was the man who had been banned from entering a church until he had repented for his sins, and his excommunication, ordered at the beginning of the summer, had been lifted. And here he was, at his grandmother's funeral. Michael's palms grew damp, and he crossed himself, hoping the Lord would understand that it was impossible for a boy of twelve to enforce the commands of the holy church, much as he might want to.

The men ended their conversation. The time had almost come for the Blessed Sacrament. The peace tablet was passed around, and the churchgoers kissed the image of the Savior, one by one, to show a willingness for peace and harmony with their neighbors. The congregation moved and many accepted the Body of Christ, though not all: some had yet to go to confession that year. The monk retreated, and Michael lost sight of him as he was carried forward by the crowd. Finally he reached the grave, which was not very deep, probably being directly above the coffins of Sigridur's parents and siblings. Rumor had it that many people who had attended their funeral services thirty years before had died of the great plague a short while later, some of them even collapsing and coughing up blood en route from the church.

The coffin was laid in the ground. Small bits of earth tumbled from the sides of the grave onto the oak lid. Michael looked down on it. He felt sad, but did not cry, and he was proud of that. He was now standing next to Thorsteinn and glanced sideways at him, a bit awkwardly, but the lawman did not look at him. His face, marked with deep lines, seemed to be carved out of stone, until the priests began to sing "*Requiem aeternam dona eis, Domine.*" At that moment his eyes came to life and filled with tears that began to roll down his rugged cheeks, along lines carved by time and grief, like brooks that find their way down craggy mountain slopes. The boy was embarrassed and glanced around swiftly to see if anyone else had noticed, but no one was looking. Summoning all his courage, he slipped his small hand into Thorsteinn's large one. The lawman kept his gaze firmly fixed on his wife's coffin, but his rough, warm palm enclosed the boy's hand and pressed it tightly. Thus they stood until the requiem ended.

❖

Ragna had no time that day or the next to mourn her mother's death. She had to look after the funeral reception for over a hundred people and to give the servants their orders. Her foster-father was not in a good state, and neither was Kristin—both of them distracted and upset. Moreover, she needed to make arrangements concerning their belongings for the voyage, as their day of departure was swiftly approaching. Most of what she would take with her—household items and textiles—was at Akrar, but she would have to go to Holar to explain the situation to Bishop Craxton and fetch their things—their duvets, clothing, and other small items. It was nearly three o'clock in the morning on Saturday when the last guests finally took their leave and she could shut the door to her mother's sleeping quarters. At last she had peace and quiet to search through Sigridur's trunks for the cloths and linens that she would take with her as her inheritence and dowry. In a modest trunk with copper clasps, she found the embroidered textiles from her formerly planned marriage to Thorkell. They were all carefully folded together with sweet-scented vernal grass laid between them. At the top of the trunk was a small chest with a lid. Opening it, she found a silver filigree hair adornment, inlaid with glittering stones. It was the Akrar family bridal tiara, most recently worn by Kristin, two years earlier. Before she knew it, she had put it on and had the contents of the trunk laid out on the floor, all the textiles with the delicately embroidered R and T, encircled with green leaves and colorful entwines. Beneath the letters was the number 1420—the year the wedding was to have taken place, embroidered in gold thread. She ran a finger over the material. On a small white cloth, she found a rust-brown stain: a drop of blood that she had never been able to wash out. She had stung herself with the needle the first time she felt Michael move in her belly.

The door opened behind her, but she took no notice, immersed as she was in painful memories.

"So do you plan to unravel my initial and sew another one in its place?"

Ragna looked up quickly. Thorkell's voice was filled with hurt and anger, like his expression.

"I don't know. Maybe," she replied self-consciously, fumbling to remove the tiara from her head. Of course he would have been informed about what was ahead. Thorsteinn had mentioned the wedding at the funeral service and told many of the guests about Sigridur's last request—for her daughter to be secure in marriage as soon as possible. In quick succession the women had offered her their condolences and in the same breath had wished her a happy, prosperous life in Greenland. Their curiosity ill-concealed, they had asked about her intended: Who was this

Valur Hauksson of Hvalsey? Who were his people? What were his holdings? Smiling timidly, she had referred their questions to her foster-father—she knew so little of the man; it had all happened so quickly.

"You cannot leave me!" He came striding toward her and knelt down, the textiles lying all around them. He took her hands in his and pressed them hard. "Thorsteinn must not separate us, Ragna, I cannot allow it. You must be strong, not weak. You are a grown woman now, yet you might as well be a child while you allow others to make your plans for you."

She was offended. "You know that he controls all my affairs. How can I rise up against that which has always been—and why should I?! I have assurance that Michael will be adopted and given the right to inherit. Don't you think that matters to me?"

"Of course it matters, but can you honestly say it matters more than our love for each other?" His dusky blue eyes looked deep into her own, yearning, searching, questioning. She knew she still loved him, and she shook her head, no. How could anything matter more than the two of them?

"What else can I do?" she asked despairingly. "There is no way out for us, you know that as well as I do. Why do you come here to torment me when you know there is nothing to be done?"

"Of course there is something to be done," he said fervently. "There is always something to be done. You must learn to have courage, Ragna. Come to Grenjadarstadur with me, where we can be together. Where we can stand together, against all the rest."

She shook her head. "I have always been frightened. I fear people's anger, deeply and desperately. I've been afraid of Thorsteinn's anger and my mother's anger, the anger of the priests, the bishops, and of almighty God. Sometimes I have even been afraid of you. I'm not strong enough to oppose Thorsteinn or to betray the promise I gave my mother on her deathbed."

"Desperate measures are not the same as a promise, Ragna. And you don't have to be strong. Just be brave, and the Lord will make you strong." Thorkell brought her hands to his lips and kissed them. "Bravery is facing your fears and taking action in spite of them. I fear the battle ahead, but I won't let cowardice prevent me from doing what is right. Even though I fear death more than anything else—I, who wish to live longer than other men. In due course, all will be different. Believe me, Ragna."

"I don't understand you, Thorkell," she said, baffled. "You speak so strangely."

He lowered his voice and glanced around furtively, like he feared someone might be nearby, listening. "In two days' time I will summon a large group of men to Enni, Magistrate Bjorn Eyjolfsson's farm, who will seek and capture the villains who have marauded through the districts this summer. The foreigner at Holar has given them shelter, and no help can be expected from either him or the king who sits on his throne on the other side of the ocean. We must seek our own revenge. We have no other choice."

Ragna drew a quick breath. "Dear Lord, Thorkell—a hand-ful of farmers are not capable of taking on English murderers and pirates! Why has the magistrate not made plans to capture those men himself? You will lead them down an evil path to their deaths—you, a priest, ordained by the Holy Ghost to do God's work!"

He smiled, and when he spoke he spoke slowly, like she was a small, upset child who did not fully comprehend what was being said. "The magistrate is useless. He is undermanned, gutless, and a drunkard. It is precisely because I am a man of God that I must do this; you know there is no one better than I around these districts to rally men to action and bolster their courage. Yes, indeed, they are farmers and tenants, salt of the earth, unused to battles other than those against dung heaps and brushwood. Yet they are strong men; all their lives they have cut and felled with spades and axes, so why would they not know how to wield a sword, if that is what it takes for them to live with some semblance of dignity. We must drive away the hooligans, to rid this land of robbers and murderers. And you need not fear that I will carry arms; that alone would have me excommunicated. I can carry our emblem and mobilize the troops—that is not forbidden in canon law, to the best of my knowledge." Thorkell reached out and stroked Ragna's cheek gently, like he could not bear not to touch her. Slowly he trailed his fingers down her throat and along the low neck of her dress. "Many of those men have waited a long time to take on the English. Particularly those who have spent the entire summer at Klifshagi, in Oxarfjord, with my old friend Father Jon Palsson."

"Father Jon? Have you enlisted his allegiance?" Ragna stared at Thorkell, astonished.

He nodded, pleased. "Jon Palsson is prepared to lay aside our differences in return for a chance to give the English their comeuppance. A few winters ago, he barely escaped alive from certain dealings with the English, and he has longed to avenge that humiliation. And I do not fear the wrath of your foster-father. He is too old to ride with us, but he supports our actions. When all is said and done, even the bishop of Holar will have to submit to my will." He embraced her, tenderly and lovingly. "I know that you are on my side, dearest. Last winter you promised that you would never betray me. Do you recall our blood oath, my love?"

Ragna assented quietly. How could she forget? Exhausted, she placed her head on Thorkell's broad chest, longing for rest and safety, for peace in her heart. Could anything she did or said change that which would come? Could she do anything but trust him? Wasn't everything planned a long, long time ago, without her involvement?

"I was planning to go to Holar tomorrow to resign as house-keeper and collect my belongings," she said, her voice half stifled. "What do you want me to do?"

Thorkell was silent. "Stick to that plan," he finally said. "I will be spending the night at Enni tomorrow with my men, and Father Jon will come the following day. I will fetch you in Hjaltadalur Valley tomorrow night. I'll wait for you after nightfall, near the brook just below Kot. You can stay at Enni while we go out on the search. The magistrate will not mind."

"But what about Michael?"

He frowned. "I cannot trust the boy to keep quiet about our plans. Our lives are at stake. No word must get to Holar."

"I go nowhere without my son," she said impulsively. "I am the only person he can rely on in this world."

"He has good relatives, too," Thorkell replied. "Why not send him to Holl tomorrow with your sister and her in-laws? He can stay with her at Hofdastrond those few days until you are meant to sail. You can have them transport the items that you plan to take with you, and when all is done we can fetch the boy, as well as your belongings. Your brother-in-law Helgi rides with us against the English, and he will hardly oppose this."

Ragna stroked one of the small cloths she had found in the chest and ran her index finger over the ornately embroidered T. "Michael would be safer with Kristin, not knowing what is to pass until the final day," she said, more to herself than to Thorkell.

"He is so reserved and has a quick temper. I can never know how he will react."

"And so, it will all end as it was originally meant to." Thorkell picked up the tiara from the floor and placed it on Ragna's head. She saw the glittering of the precious stones reflected in the depths of his eyes, and her face lit up in a smile. Surely she was dreaming; soon she would wake up in her own bed. He grasped her tightly and reached under her skirt with his hand; the tiara tumbled from her head and rolled to the middle of the floor. They lay down in each other's arms on the bed-curtain, paying no attention to anything else; it had been so long, so very long, since they were one.

Their lovemaking was intense, and the moment Ragna's body trembled in orgasm she began to sob, deeply and painfully. Thorkell pulled back, astonished. What had upset her so much? But she could not answer, did not know the answer. She didn't know why she was crying.

KISS ME, MY TRUE LOVE

———————————■———————————

Michael was having trouble holding back tears as he rode down the lane from Akrar, among the last riders in a long line that was headed out of Blonduhlid. It was as though it had first dawned on him that he was leaving for good when his grandfather Thorsteinn said good-bye to him with a firm embrace and a kiss on each cheek. He would probably never see him or Akrar again, any more than his grandmother Sigridur, who was now lying in the earth below stone slabs in the church floor. Behind them the bells of Akrar church rang out a farewell, the heavy ringing resounding in his ears long after the farm had disappeared. They had all been to morning mass and received Father Pall's blessing prior to leaving. The sound of the bells seemed filled with sadness now, even though in the past he had always found it beautiful, clear and joyful. The temperature had taken a dive in the early hours of this day of the Lord, bringing the first frost of the season, and the fields were covered in white rime. A wafer-thin, transparent sheet of ice covered the surface of the well. The stained glass in the church windows was adorned with frosted ferns in the dawn, glittering like tiny stars when the cold September sun shone on them through the arched glass.

He took some comfort in the fact that he would be staying with Kristin at Holl until they sailed for Greenland. At the same time, his heart felt heavy, watching his tiny cousin sleeping soundly in the arms of Einhildur, the wet nurse. It would not be him who would teach Ingvaldur to carve arrows, to shoot a bow, to swing a wooden sword. At first he had been sick with jealousy: this little baby would inherit countless acres of property and thousands of heads of livestock, all because he had been born in holy wedlock. He, meanwhile, would receive nothing, having been born a bastard. But all that would change now. Michael's spirits lifted slightly when he thought of all that lay ahead, and anyway, how could anyone not love a tiny imp like the ever-ravenous Ingvaldur, with his large, innocent eyes and toothless smile?

Einhildur, who rode a short distance ahead of Michael with the infant, slowed her horse, like she had sensed his thoughts. They rode side by side. She smiled warmly at him, all rosy cheeks and wholesomeness. Her blonde hair was gathered into two thick braids that danced on her back with each step of the horse. He smiled awkwardly back. Einhildur was not much older than he was. She was fresh-faced and petite, and despite the tribulation of having given birth to a stillborn child only a few weeks earlier, she had a perpetual smile on her face, especially when she had the child at her breast. A strange thrill passed through Michael, and he blushed with shame. At seeing her feed Ingvaldur, he had desperately wanted to take his cousin's place and lie against her swollen, milky-white breasts.

The riders parted ways when they came to Vidvik district. Father Thorkell, Magistrate Bjorn, Helgi Gudnason, and their entourage headed eastward toward Enni. Ragna rode on through Hrisskogur woods over the mountain ridge to Hjaltadalur, along with Klaengur the captain and a few other sailors who planned to transport goods from the bishopric to Greenland. Kristin, her in-laws, Einhildur, and Michael continued riding north along Hofdastrond.

From the ford in the Kolbeinsa River, the travelers could see the blue-green Skagafjord gleaming in the fall sunshine. Near the mouth of the river, four ships with sails rigged were moored. Three of them were late-season English vessels with their snow-white cloths wafting gently in the breeze, loaded down with stock-fish and stones from the shoreline for ballast; they would later be used to pave the streets of harbor towns on the other side of the ocean. The fourth, which was also the largest, was *Christopher* of Hull, owned by Thorsteinn Olafsson and captained by Klaengur the Red. It was tarred black, with castles at the front and back, a massive mainmast and lower mizzenmast, sails rigged on the crosstrees. A few crowing ravens glided overhead, their hoarse croaking carrying a long way in the cold sea air.

"One day, Michael, son of Ragna, from Hvalsey in the Eastern Settlement will be captain of this ship," said the boy to himself. He straightened his back and his chest widened with anticipation and pride about the heroic life that awaited him on the oceans and in the unexplored lands beyond.

It was well past noon when they rode up to Holl. The dogs leapt up to greet them, barking and yapping ecstatically as though welcoming their owners back from the dead. They were so eager that Gudni had to loudly scold them and snap his whip to curb their excitement, and even that was barely enough to settle them down. Einhildur rushed into the kitchen to tend to little Ingvaldur, who had been edgy during the second half of the journey. Michael followed her. He'd had the misfortune of getting his pant legs wet when they crossed the Hofsa River, and his feet were freezing. The kitchen was warm with a cheerful fire burning in the hearth. The delicious smell of boiling lamb rose from a pot on the fire. Yet there was an odd silence, and none of the domestics could be seen. Something was not right. Einhildur called out along the corridor for the girls to find something dry to put on the baby, but there was no answer. She shook her head, surprised, and unbuttoned her blouse, freeing her ample breasts to feed Ingvaldur, who stopped complaining as soon as the warm milk flowed down his throat and into his belly.

Suddenly a commotion could be heard, and a woman shrieked. Old Thorbjorg, perhaps. The barking of the dogs grew louder, and they heard a man's voice shouting curses, then unknown voices and the kicking of hooves. Another woman cried out; yes, it was Thorbjorg. A few moments later came the sound of people in the corridor. Michael stared at the door, petrified. Einhildur seized his shoulder roughly, dragged him to a trunk bench with a lid, and opened it.

"Get in. Now!"

He hesitated. "What about you?"

"NOW!" she hissed and shoved him into the trunk, slamming the lid so quickly that it banged on his head. Although it hurt, he lifted the lid just a touch and saw Einhildur turning in circles in the middle of the floor, still holding the baby at her breast. Then she seemed to find the way to safety—the door to the pantry was open. She managed to shut it just as the kitchen door was thrown open. A group of men entered, dressed in armor, with helmets on their heads and their swords held high. Instantly Michael doubled up inside the trunk bench, allowing the lid to close all the way. They were English, he could tell that much from their talking, which was mostly cursing and swearing. Judging by the ruckus, they were looking for something to eat and were overjoyed to find the fat slabs of meat in the pot; such delicacies they had not enjoyed in a long while. Benches and chests were dragged across the floor, and to Michael's horror one of the men plopped himself down on the trunk bench above him.

And then...the sound of a crying baby from the pantry. Michael thought his heart would stop beating. Or maybe they simply knew that the door to the pantry had been open a short while earlier and that someone must have closed it; they would have looked in there sooner or later, even if little Ingvaldur had not started crying when he had drained the breast of milk.

Einhildur shouted angrily, the infant wailed loudly, there was a commotion, and then a thud. For one instant, all was quiet. Then the agonized scream of the wet nurse sliced through the thick air inside the closed bench. One of the men laughed and said something the boy could not understand. Michael shoved his fingers into his ears, bit his teeth together so that his jaws hurt, and squeezed his eyes shut, but to no avail; he heard Einhildur's dress being torn, heard her anguished crying, and knew what the men were doing to her. Bitter gall filled his mouth, and he desperately needed to pee. Shaking with terror, he felt the warm urine begin to trickle and then flow down his thighs. *Pater noster, pater noster*, he recited silently in his mind and somehow managed to clasp his hands together, but however much he tried, he could not remember what came next in the Lord's Prayer, *pater noster, pater noster...*

Finally, after a long while, Einhildur went silent, and Michael realized that he was sobbing. Quickly he covered his mouth, but it was too late. The lid of the bench was jerked open, and he looked straight into the eyes of Oswald Miller, who stood above him with a pike, poised to strike. The sailor stared at him, astonished, hesitated one moment, then lowered the pike and dropped the lid with a loud thud.

"There's nothing there, just a squeaking mouse," he heard Oswald say loudly to his mates. "Let's go, there's nothing more to take."

Just a squeaking mouse. Yes, a mouse that just pissed itself with fear.

⟨◈⟩

The dusky evening sky over Hjaltadalur was tinged red with the rays of a setting sun. Thorkell had told Ragna to meet him after dark, but it was only just twilight. All the halls were illuminated and many people were still about, even though it was near nightfall. Ragna had excused herself from the dinner table as soon as possible, claiming she was exhausted and that she wanted to rest for the long voyage ahead. She finished packing her things in the women's quarters and then lay down, fully clothed, pulling a large woolen cover over herself. She had not been untruthful about the exhaustion, but despite that she did not fear falling asleep—she was too anxious for that.

She had found lying to Craxton difficult, and had been so reticent and halting at their meeting in the great hall that Klaengur had ended up speaking on her behalf. He had explained the situation and the need to sail as soon as possible, since the route to Greenland would soon be impassable until next summer. The bishop interpreted her silence to mean that she was much opposed to the marriage and was both understanding and kind, praising her for respecting her parents' wishes. That made her feel even worse. She could barely look at him as he wished her the very best in the most amiable manner, and before she left, he paid her even more than the salary that he owed her.

She had been quick to pack their things. Their duvets and clothing fitted on one horse and were ready in a pannier in the tack storehouse. All she had to do was to put a saddle blanket and packsaddle on the horse and tighten the girth. She would be doing it for the first time herself, though she had watched others do it often enough.

She heard the girls enter the hall and retire, one by one. Only a thin panel separated her from them, and though she could not make out any words, she could hear them whispering to each other in the dusk. She did recognize one pealing, bright laugh, however, and pressed her lips together. What on earth did Gudrun have to laugh about, one child hanging onto her apron strings and another about to burst out of her, while the father ignored them. Ragna counted the weeks on her fingers; Gudrun was so big that surely she was due within two or three weeks, at the most. That meant the baby would have been conceived…at Christmas or New Year's? She sighed deeply and squeezed her eyes shut, but to no avail: they lay in a hot embrace behind her eyelids, Gudrun laughing. May the devil take her and Thorkell too!—Even though she loved him.

An hour later, all was quiet. She waited until she heard snoring, then slipped out of bed, threw a thick wool cape over herself, and tied a triangular scarf over her head. The night would be chilly. She was able to get outside and away from the buildings without anyone seeing her—save for the dogs, who went quiet as soon as they recognized her. They followed her out to the fields to fetch her horse and back up to the storehouses. There she shooed them away, fearing they might attract attention. The tack storehouse was locked, but she still had a set of keys and soon found the one that fit. She had little trouble putting the packsaddle on the horse and tightening the girder, but she found it somewhat harder to put up the packs and fasten them. Her hands were not particularly strong, and she almost wanted to give up, but she managed it in the end and was able to lead the horse out of the storehouse and down into the valley.

The still moon shone a cold light on the red rocks of Mt. Holabyrda and the path in front of her. Ragna gazed up at the starry sky and spotted Frigg's Spinning Wheel in the southern sky, the ancient goddess of marriage and fertility. Neither were intended for her, apparently. And anyway, Frigg was not someone she believed in, but rather Holy Mary, Mother of God. She crossed herself again with her head lowered, feeling ashamed to have wasted a thought on a heathen idol. She walked with quick steps, the horse willingly allowing itself to be led behind her, despite being more accustomed to carrying a rider than a pack. When they crossed the Hjaltadalur River, she clambered onto its back and sat sideways atop her luggage; even though the icy water was shallow, it might reach above her boots, and she did not care to get her feet wet in such frost. Even though the route was not very long and she was warmly dressed, she was numb with cold by the time she reached the brook below Kot. Immensely relieved, she knelt at the edge of the hot pool and soaked her hands, which were already blue with cold, in the warm water. Steam wafted up from the brook, enveloping the nearby surroundings in a mist. There was complete silence, broken not even by the distant chirp of a bird or a bleating sheep. Thick clouds were piling up in the sky, and it was dreadfully cold. A cloud covered the moon, and the darkness deepened. In that black silence, Ragna shuddered and reached inside her cape for the small silver cross that she wore around her neck, softly murmuring the Angelus: "*Ave Maria gratia plena, Dominus tecum…*"

Finally: the sound of hooves. As he approached it was almost like the white horse had no rider, the man merged so well with the darkness, dressed in a black cloak with a hood. He leapt from his horse and walked to greet her, smiling, his arms outstretched, waiting to gather her in an embrace. She was enormously relieved to see him.

He had expected her to be on horseback and had not taken along another horse, so they had to ride double on his regal steed. Her own horse with the panniers lagged behind, tied to the tail of Thorkell's horse. They rode slowly, but Ragna didn't mind; it was good to have him so close, his strong arms around her, holding the reins. She tightened the cape around her and nestled closer to him. The chill was gone from her bones, and the journey could take all night for all she cared.

Before she knew it, they were over Hrishals Pass and into the birch woods behind it. The horses plodded through yellow and red leaves that reached up to their fetlocks. The wind picked up, whistling in the crowns of the trees and whipping faded leaves from the ground so they swirled around them. Ragna wanted to ask about what lay ahead. Would the group leave Enni as early as tomorrow morning to search for the English, and did he absolutely have to go with them? After all, he was a priest, and wouldn't it make more sense to ride directly to Grenjadarstadur? But she held her peace, knowing that her questions would only trouble him and make him angry. It was pointless now to tell him about the blood-red moon above Hjaltadalur; everything would turn out as it was supposed to.

They rode on in silence. Thorkell began to sing quietly, next to her ear. She listened to his dim voice, surprised and happy:

Kiss me, my true love
The hour will surely come

When we will not see
The sun, together as one
Our enemies are kin
Cousins, mine and yours.
May they all be thwarted
Who wish to see us part.

Michael's back hurt terribly from the weight of the sack he carried. With each step of the horse, the straps cut into his shoulders, and his crotch burned where his damp pants chafed against his skin. Yet he did not slow his horse or attempt to adjust the sack; the only thing he could think of was to get to his destination as soon as possible, away from the pool of blood on the kitchen floor and the agony in Einhildur's lifeless, staring eyes. The horse trotted the entire length of the Hofdastrond coast, past one farm after another, that he could just barely make out in the dusk. He never stopped, except to rest his horse for a few short moments at the rivers while he tried to remember landmarks and find the fords that they had crossed over a few hours earlier. The moon lit his way for the first part of the journey, but then clouds began to gather and covered it. The wind picked up. He peered into the black night. What if it started snowing, would that make it easier for the men to follow him? Oh, but surely Oswald would not let them. Oswald Miller was his friend. He repeated the statement a few times to himself and felt slightly better afterward, then spoke the words into the night: "Oswald Miller is my friend!" His own voice, cutting through the silence, startled him. It sounded croaky and strange, and he was afraid he might have woken the baby. But Ingvaldur remained quiet, and he was relieved; it was best if his little cousin could sleep for the entire journey.

Finally, finally he arrived at the Kolbeinsa River and directed the horse downward; the ford was a short distance from the mouth. He could just make out the ships in the harborage, but only because he knew they were there. He could see a lantern in the dark, moving along like it was gliding over the sea. The surf droned as it hit the nearby shore, and the air smelled of seaweed and salt. Halfway across the river, it occurred to him that the men might be there, very near, in the dark; perhaps they had not headed north, but rather back to the ship. Maybe he had been riding behind them the entire time and nothing but God's grace had prevented them from taking notice of him. At that thought, Michael kicked the side of the horse so hard that it started, and he nearly fell into the icy cold river. He managed to grab hold of the mane and held on for dear life until the horse had reached the other side, both of them shaking from the cold. He dismounted and patted the horse soothingly, speaking to it softly, his speech coming in spasms in the sub-zero temperatures. "There, there boy, of course they're not here, and they wouldn't see us anyway if they were because it is so dark. Little Ingvaldur is not afraid. He isn't even crying. There is nothing to be afraid of anyway." In that way he managed to overcome most of the chills and clattering of teeth; he was able to clamber back onto the horse and continue on his way. From there he only needed to cross the shallow Hjaltadalur River, and then it was only a short distance to Enni.

◈

They had only just dismounted in the farmyard when they saw the boy coming. His horse seemed fatigued yet began trotting up the bridle path, knowing that some hay and much longed-for rest was not far off. The dogs ran, barking and yelping, to greet the boy. Michael sat slumped over in the saddle, almost like he was sleeping, and appeared neither to see nor hear when Ragna called out to him. She helped him dismount and then asked what in God's name he was doing there all alone. He looked at his mother with a vacant expression in his eyes and made no answer. He was barely able to stand without help. It wasn't until she started loosening the sack that he carried on his back that he began to talk, and then the words streamed from his mouth so rapidly that they had trouble understanding him: "Ingvaldur has been sleeping for so long, and he's hungry. Einhildur can't feed him anymore because she's…and Kristin is gone because the Englishmen took her, all of them except Gudni and Thorbjorg, and they didn't answer. Oswald helped me. Maybe they're dead, so I left and took Ingvaldur, but he hasn't woken up, and he must be so hungry… he just sleeps and sleeps…"

Thorkell grabbed him by the shoulders. "What are you saying, boy?! Englishmen?! Did they come to Holl? Where did they go? Try to speak sense!"

At that Michael clammed up and stared at him in despair. Ragna pushed Thorkell aside and put her arms around her son. "Tell us, darling," she said, calmly and quietly. "You're safe now. Where is little Ingvaldur?"

The boy pointed to the sack on the ground. Ragna was gripped by dread. With trembling hands she untied the sack and gasped when she touched Ingvaldur's silky smooth cheek, moist and icy cold.

"Dear Lord help us!" she whispered and crossed herself. "They have spared no one!"

"No, no, he's just sleeping!" Michael cried and was about to fall on his knees next to the baby's corpse, but Thorkell held him back. Michael thrashed about, trying to free himself, and then suddenly stopped resisting and went limp in Thorkell's arms, leaned against him, and began to sob uncontrollably.

The barking of the dogs, or the sobbing, or perhaps both, alerted the Enni residents to the new arrivals. Bjorn the magistrate came out holding a torch, and more men followed. The flame cast a light on the faces of the people, and the magistrate bid them welcome in God's name. That same moment there was a shout. Helgi Gudnason from Holl had seen his firstborn child lying on the ground, and he leapt forward, scooping his son up in his arms. Ingvaldur's small head rolled lifelessly to one side; there was a large, dark stain at the back of his neck. Helgi let out a strange, choking sound. He stared at his son in disbelief, then at Michael, still sobbing in Thorkell's arms.

"What happened, boy?" he asked, his voice strained. "Where are Kristin and my parents?"

Michael sniffled and tried to answer but could not speak an intelligible word.

"They were attacked by the English," said Thorkell. "They may have abducted some people, and I fear that some may have been killed." He shook Michael. "Try to calm yourself, boy, and tell us how many there were. Where did they attack? Was it on the way to Holl?"

The boy shook his head. "When we got there..." he hiccupped. "Lots of them, I don't know, a dozen or maybe more...I hid till they were gone."

The men had been standing quietly in front of the house, but now they all began to speak at once. Most wanted to set off in pursuit of the English immediately, north along Hofdastrond. The longer they waited, the likelier it was that the villains would escape. They might even make it to their ship with the people and the goods. The air was filled with their nervous chatter until Bjorn the magistrate put up his hand and in a loud voice asked the men to keep calm and let him speak.

"We do not know how many English there are, nor where they have headed to from Holl," he said. "No doubt they are well armed; it has been my experience that those English dogs are skilled in battle, as many of you know. Jon Palsson has sent thirty men who are expected to arrive from Oxarfjord in the morning. I suggest we wait for them and for daybreak. It is impossible to follow any sort of trail in this darkness."

Helgi Gudnason, still holding his son's body, shook his head. "No," he said gruffly. "Every minute counts. If we leave now, we'll reach Holl at daybreak, and then we'll be able to follow their tracks. We are more than thirty and all dressed for battle. Jon Palsson and his men would make a good addition, but we don't have time to wait."

The magistrate was clearly not pleased with the opposition but did not protest. It was evident from the faces of those present that they sided with Helgi.

Thorkell spoke. "You both have a point, but the best thing would be to ambush the English, if at all possible, before they can inflict more damage. Besides, we may well meet Jon Palsson and his troop as we travel north on Hofdastrond. Either that or those English villains will, should they have continued north."

"All right," said the magistrate curtly. "Let us prepare for the journey."

TO EVERYTHING THERE IS A SEASON

Fear begins at the nape of the neck, settles in, and makes the hairs stand on end. Then it trickles down the spine and sets all muscles on the alert, preparing them to fight or flee when the body is face-to-face with an antagonist. It also seeps into the chest, making the heart beat faster and the breath come in spurts.

Thorkell Gudbjartsson ran a gloved hand down the back of his neck, tightening his cloak around him. He shivered, despite the thick, stiff leather armor of cowhide, lent to him by the magistrate, that he wore beneath the heavy wool of his cloak. On a broad chain around his neck, he wore a large silver-lined rood; perhaps the English might show respect for a crucified Christ, even if they did not spare infants. Though that was far from certain.

Heading up the procession were Helgi, Bjorn the magistrate, and Thorkell, unarmed but carrying an emblem for the troop, as he had promised Ragna. That emblem had caught everyone's attention, and the men had looked at one another in some surprise, for they knew it, even though it was ancient. It had twelve stripes, the number of the Icelandic districts, alternating silver and blue. Missing, however, was the red lion of the Kingdom of Norway, holding an axe in its claws, which had been placed over the Icelandic colors for over a hundred and fifty years. Yet no one remarked on this, not even the king's magistrate, who occasionally gave the emblem—and its carrier—a worried glance, looking a bit like he'd eaten something very sour but was trying his best to swallow it anyway.

The heavy clouds had been swept away from the moon, so they were able to find their way fairly easily. Helgi led the group, holding a torch and keeping a vigilant eye on the trail ahead, a grim expression on his face. The mail shirts of the men who rode near the front reflected the light from the flame, and a low clamor merged with the sound of hooves, as sword holsters, pikes, cross-bows, and quivers clashed with armor, breastplates, and brigan-dines. Some of the men carried gauntlets and even metal helmets that they had bought from the English. Others wore old home-made helmets, without rims, with protection extending down between the eyes and over the nose. Some of them hardly had any protection—they were farmhands, armed only with wood axes and their own physical strength.

Here and there on the trail, they spotted fresh horse manure, which could have been dropped by the horses of the Holl people the day before—or anyone else's, for that matter. At any rate, there wasn't enough to signal that more than six or seven horses had passed that way.

Having forded the Hofsa River, Thorkell signaled for the men to stop. Daybreak loomed on the horizon. The night would soon be gone.

"From here it is only a short distance to Holl," he said. "Evidently the English have not yet boarded their ship. They probably decided to rest overnight, and they cannot be far away. I should think it best for two men to go ahead: one down to Hofdavatn Lake, the other the shortest route along the mountain slope to Holl. They can have a quick look around. If we're in luck, we can catch them unaware."

The men looked at each other uncertainly. Who was willing to go ahead? Thorkell glanced around and waited a few moments. "I'll go to Holl," he said when no one volunteered.

Helgi shook his head. "No. I'll go. You go down to the lake," he said.

Thorkell nodded in agreement. "Let us meet back here within the hour." He rode to a large boulder, loosened two bags that were hitched on each side of his pommel, and placed them on the rock. He handed the emblem to Bjorn, who took it from him with a sullen expression. It was best to have as little as possible with him, should he need to take off at a gallop.

"Don't touch the packs," he warned the group, then drove his spurs into the sides of his horse and bolted into the dusky light of the morning.

This was the day.

He slowed his horse as he approached Hofdavatn Lake, glanced around, but saw no sign of men or horses. There was old manure on the trail leading to the low turf farm south of the lake; no one could have gone there in the last few days. A frosty vapor hovered above the large lake, wrapping the surroundings in a gloomy mist and hiding the Hofdabaer farm just beyond it. The great cliffs of Gusthnjukur peak, above Holl, were just visible. There was no sound, save for the occasional squawking of birds on the lake. He heard the chilly laugh of the Great Northern Diver. Livestock slept in the fields; nothing amiss there. The English must have headed northward from Holl, along the side of the mountain. Thorkell hesitated a brief moment, then headed onward into the band of fog that lay low over the land. He pricked up his ears in the silence. It was probably most sensible to head toward Holl; it would be easier to trace the path of the

English from there. His horse appeared to sense the tension of its rider and yanked its head, champing at the bit.

Heading up the small foothill between the borders of Holl and Vatn, Thorkell's horse stopped and refused to go further. Thorkell urged it on, impatiently. It would not budge. At that same moment, he heard the sound of men's voices coming from the darkness. Were they speaking English or Nordic? He leapt from his horse and walked over to the slope with his head down, then fell on his hands and knees and crawled the last bit of the way. On the other side of the slope was a large, deep basin. Six tents formed a circle around a pyre. To the east of the tents, closer to the mountain, there was a group of horses. Three guards meandered about on the slope, talking gibberish. He caught the odd word; it was English. It sounded like they were bickering. One of them was holding a large ferrule with a wooden handle over his shoulder. A culverin. Thorkell cursed under his breath.

He crawled slightly closer on his belly. Each tent could contain five or six men. Where was that godforsaken Father Jon now and his thirty brave men who had promised to come to Enni this Monday morning? Had they deceived him? He wiped beads of sweat from his brow and turned. Those English villains would get a rude awakening, with or without Jon Palsson.

A few moments later, he came upon Helgi on the trail below Holl. Kristin was with him, seemingly unhurt, although there was blood splattered on her dress. Helgi had found her hiding inside the barn, terrified.

"What about the others—the old couple and the domestics?" asked Thorkell. Helgi looked despondently at the mountain, avoiding his pitying, inquisitive gaze. "Dead. All of them," he said in a husky voice.

Kristin's shoulders shook with silent sobs, and her hands trembled. At first she could respond to their questions only in single syllables, but before long they were able to get the full story. She had taken her horse up to the storage shed and had just finished removing the saddle when she heard screaming and saw the men attack the old couple with axes in front of the house. She had not seen where they came from, everything had happened so fast, but they must have been hiding behind one of the farm buildings and waiting for them to arrive. She had run into the storage shed and nearly tripped over the bodies of the domestics who lay on the floor, near the door. At that dreadful sight she had fainted. No doubt this had saved her, for when she came to, she heard one of the Englishmen come into the storeroom to look for survivors. She had not dared to stir—perhaps she had not even been able to—but lay perfectly still, paralyzed by fear, where she had landed on top of one of the corpses. The man had gone into the attic and checked every corner, cursing and shouting. She had held her breath, and by the grace of God he had not noticed her.

"Why didn't you go for help when they were gone?" asked Helgi.

Kristin stared at the ground. "I couldn't find Ingvaldur inside," she whispered. "Maybe they took him. Einhildur was—I was too frightened..." Her voice broke, and she began to cry. Helgi put his arms around her. "Michael went to Enni for help and took Ingvaldur with him," he said softly. "Our boy..." He stopped in mid-sentence. Thorkell looked at him intently, shook his head, and put a finger to his lips. *Not now.*

"Time is of the essence," he said. "We must hurry if we want to catch the English off guard."

Kristin looked at her husband, her eyes full of tears. "You're not going to leave me?"

"Don't be afraid, my darling," Helgi replied, stroking her cheek gently. "I'll come back soon. You're safer here. In the morning, when it's all over, we'll go fetch our boy."

He kissed her forehead and swiftly mounted his horse. They rode back at a gallop.

❖

Standing on a large rock, Thorkell outlined his plan. His voice was impassioned and unwavering. Their best chance would be to ambush the English while they were in their tents sleeping. They would move quietly along the eastern slope of the mountain, make their way to the upper side of the basin, and attack before the English could seize their weapons. He lifted a vat and the pouches he'd taken along, showing them to the men. "In this we put crushed sulphur, wood coals, and saltpeter lye to create an explosion. We must kill the guards first so we can move to the east of the tents unseen."

They nodded, no longer uncertain, spurred on by his intensity.

"Which of you are most skilled with a bow?" he asked. Two young men, red-haired brothers, stepped forward. They showed their weapons, strong crossbows, cocked with short but razor-sharp metal arrows. Thorkell nodded and asked the best long-bow shooters to go ahead of them. It was safer that way; even though the crossbows had a longer range and the metal arrows penetrated deeper than wooden ones, they took a longer time to draw. Also, the large crossbows had a more precise aim.

They were about to head off when the magistrate, who had been fairly quiet until then, requested a group prayer. Could the priest not say a few words of blessing? Thorkell hesitated a moment, impatient; dawn was fast approaching. Then he agreed, aware that he should have suggested such a thing himself; after all, it gave the men strength to know that God was with them. He dismounted, and the men followed suit. Hats and helmets were removed, and the men lowered their heads. In a deep voice, Thorkell guided them in the Lord's Prayer, all the while searching his mind for the appropriate scripture. He found it in the Psalms of David and recited it in Nordic, so that they would all understand:

"Merciful Father, give us aid against the enemy, for human help is worthless. With God we will gain the victory, and He will trample down our enemies! In the name of the Father and the Son and the Holy Ghost. Amen."

Then they mounted their horses and rode off in God's name.

❖

The guards were some distance away from each other, to the east and west of the basin. One was gazing into the mist, the other sitting on his haunches fiddling with his weapon, his back turned to the mortal danger behind him. The third—the one who had held a gun over his shoulder—was nowhere to be seen. The archers crawled closer on either side of the guards, looking for a good place to take aim. The red-haired brothers had their crossbows cocked and roller nuts in place.

The rest of the men waited on the mountain slope. Silently and anxiously they watched Thorkell mix the powder he carried in his pouches: crushed sulphur and wood coals, and strange yellowish crystals that smelled like old urine. A fine dust rose from the mixture, and they flinched at the rancid stench it gave off.

Thorkell handed them a large wad of hemp to tear up and stuff into the horses' ears. The big challenge would be to restrain them when the mixture exploded.

The arrows flew from their bows. First two, side by side, and a moment later another two, cutting through the cold air with a low whoosh. One missed its target; three sank deep into flesh. The longbows were drawn again; two more arrows hit their targets. The guards collapsed on the ground, their moans barely audible. One lay still; the other rolled over and over, down the slope until it reached the horses. The ones nearest to him snorted and moved away nervously. Apart from that there was silence.

A moment later, two men were down in the basin carrying a vat. They placed it near the horses and the corpse, then returned with the metal arrow from the neck of the guard. He was barely out of his teens. A blonde-haired boy.

The brothers wrapped a hank of tow around their arrows. It was vital now to take good aim. Thorkell lit the tow, reminding the men to hold firmly onto the horses and to sling shield-straps over their shoulders. The shots had to be taken at the same instant the explosion happened.

The whoosh of arrows once more. This time they glided high and far, but the flame went out on one before it hit the ground. No matter: the other one hit the vat, flames surged up, and a deafening noise crashed against their eardrums, horrifying and terrible. Blue and red lightning bolts shot out of the vat, and everything was enveloped in a great cloud of smoke. The nauseating smell of sulphur filled the air. At the very same instant, the horses bolted, kicking and rearing, wild with terror. They galloped in all directions, over tents, here and there and back again, up the slope towards them.

For a few moments, the men were paralyzed by the noise. The frantic horses tugged at the reins, desperately trying to get away. Suddenly they all bolted down the slope into the basin. The sounds of galloping hooves merged with a blast that never seemed to end. Hooves crushed both tents and men, swords flew into the air, goads were embedded, half-dressed, defenseless Englishmen rushed around shouting, crying out for their God, begging for mercy. But alas, God had other business to attend to that morning. Wild horses maimed and killed as many as wild men did. There was a blast of thunder in the midst of the mayhem, a red-blue flare flashing through the dusk. One of the Englishmen managed to fire the gun. A rider, arms flailing, fell backward and onto the ground. The angel of death glided over the battlefield with spread wings, staking its claim, its pale white countenance smeared with soot. The gunman was unable to reload; a sharp axe cut away both arm and weapon.

The sun rose over Gusthnjukur in the east. The sky burned with terrifying beauty.

◈

In the twilight before dawn, when the sky is both light and dark and the land and its inhabitants between sleeping and waking, I sense my smallness before God. Him who always prevails over night. The dark unnerves me; it holds unknown threats. Thorkell frightens me the same way; the dark worlds of his eyes contain secrets. Why am I here? Why do I allow myself feebly to be led from one place to another, thinking only of how I can be worthy in his eyes, more deserving of his affections than all the rest? I barely know myself anymore. Knowledge is power, he said. But what good is knowledge of the way things work if one does not recognize oneself, does not know one's own heart and thoughts? Did I perhaps expect him to be a coward like me, that we could hold hands and be frightened together? He is not. His world is unlike mine. It is as though he fears nothing, neither darkness nor death. He almost seems to live for both. He was dazzling when he rode to meet the English, ahead of the rest, holding our country's emblem, but he did not so much as glance at me. He never looked back, only saw what lay ahead. Unlike me, who only looks back, not daring to look at the road before me.

What if he is killed?

◈

There were more than twenty of them. Many had bruises and broken bones; some were washed in blood. Defeated men, still alive. Kristin walked past the line, glaring at each one. Some avoided her wrathful gaze, while others looked at her anxiously, a silent appeal for clemency on their faces: *At home, in Bristol, we have women who wait for us, young children, elderly parents.* One wept bitterly, like a small child; perhaps he was injured, or scared. Probably both.

She lifted a trembling hand and pointed an index finger at a short, burly, dark-haired man. That one. And this one, the one with the black teeth. She pointed her finger again and found a third: a young boy, muscular, with broad shoulders. She walked on, came to a halt in front of the gaunt and thin Oswald Miller. His cheeks were wet from crying, and he swallowed repeatedly. She hesitated, uncertain. Oswald's brown eyes darted furtively to the side, and she followed his gaze to the front of the line, seeing a middle-aged man with a black beard who stared at the ground. She nodded, her expression stony. That one too.

They took the assassins down to the gravel spit at Hofdaa River. There they untied them so they could dig graves for their dead comrades in a ling-covered basin, near the riverbank. Arduous work, this digging. The ground was mostly hard gravel, yet the grave needed to be large enough to fit a number of bodies. By the time they finished, it was nearly noon. The corpses were dumped into the grave, one on top of another.

The Englishmen looked at the man with the shaved crown and the Holyrood around his neck. The magistrate noticed.

"Would it not be fitting for the priest to say a few words over the grave of dead?" he said, ever just and God-fearing. Stealing horses and fish, slaughtering women and men, even the murder of a child changed nothing where that was concerned.

Thorkell shrugged. "They can all go to hell as far as I'm concerned," he said coldly. "Helgi, what do you think?"

Helgi Gudnason looked up from where he sat on a rock, sharpening a large axe, wearing a grim expression.

"I couldn't care less." He kept sharpening the axe. "Say what you want. Or maybe you should wait until the others are in there." He gestured towards the Englishmen. Thorkell nodded. They had been watching the exchange silently and nervously, but now it was like it dawned on them, in spite of them not understanding the foreign language.

Death was reflected in the gleaming blade of the axe.

The stocky man threw himself on his knees and shouted something in English, no doubt begging for mercy in God's name, proclaiming his innocence and shouting that he had not killed anyone. They dragged him to the rock first, the axe razor-sharp; it was over quickly. Red blood on wilted grass. Blackbeard was next. He thrashed about and the blow missed, even though they tried to hold him still. It landed on the back of his skull. The maroon stain on the ground grew larger. Bjorn the magistrate walked down to the river and vomited.

The youngest one, a dark-eyed, muscular boy, kicked and thrashed wildly. Then suddenly he was free, bolting toward the lake.

"Go, Thomas Clarke! Swim!" his comrade yelled. He was rewarded with a heavy blow to the side of the head and fell forward onto the bloody rock. The boy ran into the water and began to swim. Helgi threw the axe to one side and followed him. A pod of eider ducks scattered in confusion, and the great northern divers flew up, cackling loudly at this unexpected commotion. A trout flipped its tail in surprise and darted under the riverbank.

The Englishman swam straight ahead, but soon he seemed to realize the distance. He changed course and swam north to the narrow gravel isthmus that separated the lake from the sea. Helgi swam with strong, even strokes and gained on the Englishman, a lust for revenge coursing through his blood. Straight ahead was the great Thordarhofdi promontory: round and undulating in front, crags and slopes on the side, a sheer cliff facing the sea.

Desperation gave the Englishman unexpected energy. Back on dry land, he began to run over sea-smoothed rocks, toward the promontory, leaping over piles of kelp and pieces of driftwood that lay scattered about. Quick as a fox in flight, seemingly tireless, small drops of water spraying in all directions. As he reached the isthmus, Helgi put his hands on his knees to catch his breath, cold water streaming from his clothes and hair. Then he continued the chase, unrelenting, knowing the end was near. Above them gulls swarmed, the sound of the seabirds growing increasingly louder.

On the slope the boy needed to clamber over rocky, uneven ground, and he lost momentum. Still, he did not stop and looked neither right nor left. Not until he saw the sheer cliff ahead and realized there was no escape. White-topped waves broke at the foot of the cliff, more than a hundred and twenty yards below. Only then did he appear to realize. Slowly, hesitatingly, he turned to face his pursuer. Helgi approached with heavy steps, breathlessly, a brass-handled knife drawn and in his hand. They looked into each other's eyes. Thomas Clarke turned and jumped.

Death is insatiable, as are the netherworlds.

At the gravel spit, east of Hofdavatn, they had filled the grave. The dark voice of Father Thorkell Gudbjartsson rang out in the still morning air:

"*De terra plasmasti me et carne induisti me. Redemptor meus, Domine, resuscita me in novissimo die.*" From the earth you formed me, and out of flesh you clothed me. My redeemer, O Lord, raise me up on the last day.

FREEDOM

—————————◼—————————

They arrived in Vidvik district after nightfall that evening. Some of the prisoners were so exhausted from the long trek that they tripped over every rock and tussock. Two of the men were too battered and sore to walk, so they had been allowed to ride double on a sturdy, pied horse. The rest had walked the entire Hofdastrond coast in a long line, tied together with a rope that looped around each of their necks, their trousers soaked from wading through icy rivers. "I daresay they're not too good to travel this way, disgraced and on foot, taking the same route they previously took looting and maiming on stolen horses," said Thorkell. Residents of farms they passed came out of their houses to watch this curious procession go by—a line of prisoners flanked by armed men on horseback. The more bold among them picked up stones from the ground and threw them at the Englishmen, the odd person even coming close enough to spit.

Thorkell was furious, and the humiliation of the English gave him little comfort. Yes, his men had emerged victorious, mostly thanks to him and his thunderous explosion. Only one Icelander had been killed—the man who was shot—and three others had received minor abrasions and wounds. But Jon Palsson, the rat, had betrayed them. No one had seen him or his band of men from Oxarfjord, as had been promised. Moreover, no messages had arrived, thus it could only be surmised that he had always planned to lie to and deceive them. The battle had been won without him—yet the war was not over, and what lay ahead would be more difficult without his support and that of his followers. "May he rot in his excommunication for all eternity," said Thorkell bitterly. "And anyway, people turn against those who don't keep their word." The magistrate and the others concurred. Henceforth, Father Jon would not be trusted.

◇◈◇

The women and children stood in front of the Enni buildings and watched in wide-eyed silence as all twenty-three prisoners were led up the bridle path to the farm. Frightened children hid behind their mothers' skirts, and the women crossed themselves in the name of the Father and the Son and the Holy Ghost. So their men had triumphed over those rapists and murderers. The women who had feared for their lives and doubted their assiduousness and skill now felt ashamed of their lack of faith and smiled with nervous relief.

Michael stood next to his mother, holding a lantern. He held it high so that it would cast a better light. The English appeared defeated, the majority plodding along with their heads down, bruised and battered, staring at the ground. Some of them he recognized, including Captain Bell and Edmund Smith, who had presented the grand altarpiece to St. Mary's Cathedral. There was a bloody bandage around Bell's right thigh and he limped with every step, yet his head was held high and he gave the onlookers a harsh stare as he was led past.

The boy avoided the stinging gaze of the captain and saw another familiar face—that of Oswald Miller. His face was grimy, and he had a split upper lip and an immense black eye, though he appeared otherwise uninjured. He gazed at Michael with plead-ing eyes, his lips moved, and the boy saw rather than heard him whisper his name and ask for mercy: *"Save my life now, Michael, my lad, like I did yours!"*

The boy shuddered and wanted most of all to pretend he didn't know him and that they had never been friends. Maybe Oswald was one of those who had murdered Ingvaldur and Einhildur. He did not want to think about the fact that this man had saved his life and he had repaid him by unleashing terrible acts of vengeance against the English. Yet it was impossible for him to look away when the sailor moved slowly past. Oswald was forced to look straight ahead to see where he and his comrades were being taken, and he called out in broken Nordic, plead-ing with the kind people standing there to have mercy on these pathetic sinners, in God's name.

"We hungry, give eat?" he said in a trembling voice. His comrades stopped all at once, as though it had been planned. They stared at the women, and a few extended their palms like beggars and pointed at their mouths and stomachs; they had eaten nothing for twenty-four hours. The women looked at each other hesitatingly; yes, these men were criminals, but they were a pitiful sight to be sure, broken and tattered, with soaking wet feet. Did they deserve pity, or perhaps just a morsel of food? Someone yanked on the rope that held them together, ordering them to be quiet and to keep walking. The English dug in their heels and resisted, but they were forced to obey when the archers pointed their arrows at them with gestures that could not be misunderstood.

Michael was about to follow them, thinking it probable that they would be locked in the large storehouse to the east of the farm. Ragna put her hands on his shoulders and stopped him.

"You stay here," she said firmly. "We're going inside, and you're going to lie down and rest. You need sleep." He had not slept a wink ever since his hellish ride from Holl, could not close his eyes without the horror replaying itself behind his eyelids: Einhildur's mutilated body on the kitchen floor and the old couple lying in a pool of blood in the farmyard. His eyes would fly open the moment he closed them, and he would stare at the beam in the sloping ceiling above his bed, upset, hardly daring to blink.

One of the women snorted and remarked that thieves should be both whipped and hanged—there was no need to feed such people. Another agreed: just think of all the horses they have stolen from around the district, even from the magistrate himself. Murderers should get the axe and horse thieves should be hanged, as is written in the law of the land.

The boy followed his mother into the farm as though in a trance. He had seen a hanged person before—the girl who had killed herself in the cowshed at Holar, Brynhildur from Thufnakot. The image of her dangling body was engraved in his mind, a look of terror on her swollen, blue face. Oswald did not deserve to die like that. Surely he had not killed anyone. They were friends! He had told him stories and taught him poems in English. Maybe Oswald had even tried to stop his comrades from committing those evil deeds. Michael clenched his fists. Surely that was it. And now, he had to act with courage; he had to find a way. Only the most wretched coward would not at least try to save an innocent friend from the gallows.

❧

"What do you plan to do with the Englishmen?" Ragna directed her question to Thorkell, as his seatmate, Bjorn the magistrate, did not look likely to answer. Bjorn's lanky body was half up on the table, his hands were under his chin, and he snored loudly, even though he had only drunk about half as much ale as many of those who were still awake. Only a few of the men had ever been in battle before, and most had only seen blood spilled during the annual slaughter season. They had never before shot arrows at anything that moved, save for birds and foxes. Consequently, the magistrate's liquor supply was barely able to wipe away the blood still flowing from the veins of the dead in the men's recollection of that morning's horror. And yet the liquor seemed to amplify the thrill of their victory, and they had begun laughing and singing and toasting to each other. Many of those toasts were drunk to Thorkell Galdur of the Dark Arts and his great explosion. They chose to ignore the resentment that flickered across the priest's face when he was referred to by that unfortunate nickname.

Thorkell himself had drunk a great deal, yet it was hard to see any liquor on him. The only sign of his drunkenness was a film over his dusky blue eyes. He pushed the sleeping magistrate further away and invited Ragna to sit down between them on the bench.

"The fate of the English is in the hands of their countryman at Holar," he said, pouring ale into a drinking horn and handing it to her. She had been rushing back and forth between kitchen and hall all evening and quaffed the warm ale, thirsty from the smoke in the hearth and the heat in the crowded hall.

"What do you mean?" she asked, surprised, wiping her mouth with a corner of the tablecloth that lay in her lap. "Is it not the magistrate, rather than the bishop, who should pass a sentence over them?"

Thorkell smiled, smug and sure of his victory, his eyes twinkling. "They've already been sentenced to death by hanging, each and every one, for grand theft of fish and horses. By God's will and mine, John Williamsson Craxton shall have the option of releasing them from that sentence. He'll be able to do so by relinquishing the bishop's seat and securing their departure from this country by accompanying them himself, on a ship that is half his, by virtue of the share that he purchased a short while ago. I hope, dearest, that you have no objection to residing with me at Holar, rather than at Grenjadarstadur."

Ragna was shocked. "Thorkell! If you take the bishop's seat by force, you will be banned from all sacraments and receive eternal damnation in hell!"

He shook his head. "Dearest Ragna, what you don't understand is that I have planned all my moves very carefully. There will be no blood spilled in this battle. I would not risk my plans in that way. The pope will not appoint an Icelander to the see unless that man has the support of those who control the fish trade at any given time. Alternatively—and there is more hope for this now—he must have the support of a bishop who voluntarily renounces office and returns to his home country. After all that has transpired, Craxton will no longer be secure on the bishop's seat, and since that is the case, our only option is to seize power—without violence if at all possible, with violence if all else fails. The next bishop of Holar will be Icelandic, selected and supported by Icelanders." Thorkell caught hold of her chin and forced her to look into his eyes. He no longer appeared loving; instead, he seemed threatening, and there was fire in his eyes. "We live in times of change and upheaval, Ragna. It is every man for himself. You must now decide, simple woman, where you want to stand: with me, or against me."

His sudden change of mood shocked her, and she moved back, accidentally bumping into Magistrate Bjorn, who rolled from the bench and onto the floor with a thud. He groaned and touched his head with his hand, then turned over on his side and continued snoring beneath the table, his upper body hidden behind the tablecloth that nearly touched the floor. Thorkell raised his eyebrows scornfully. The sounds in the hall remained as before; no one paid any attention to the passed-out magistrate.

"I may be only an ignorant woman," Ragna said nervously, "but even I know that Mr. Craxton is appointed by the pope in Rome and the pope is chosen by God."

Thorkell laughed coldly. "The pope is chosen by men, cardinals, who are born as sinful as you and I. They are bought and sold like prostitutes. He himself is born of a woman, conceived in sin and lust, just like…"

"Blasphemy!" she interjected, upset. "This is madness!"

He lifted his hand swiftly, his expression furious. Instinctively she raised her arm, thinking he was going to hit her. He lowered his hand again and leaned forward so close that she felt the heat from his breath. He spoke slowly, his tone caustic:

"No, my dear Ragna Gautadottir, there is no madness in thinking differently from others and aspiring to higher things. The secret lies in daring to be different, finding strength in knowledge, and understanding things that are concealed from others. Thanks to your betrayal, I attended seminaries in both Germany and France, and one of the things I learned is that those who want to rise from the dust and become greater than the rest must dare to go after what they want. John Craxton will bend to my will, just you wait and see. Otherwise, those twenty-three men will be hanged like the robbers and thugs they are."

She looked at him, filled with despair, and did not know what, if anything, she should say. All she knew was that this would come to a terrible end.

190

◈

From his nook, Michael saw the magistrate hit the floor. He could hardly believe his luck. He waited a short while; his mother and Father Thorkell were deep in conversation and saw only each other, and the men next to them had their backs turned. He would scarcely get a better opportunity. Slowly he moved closer, without them noticing, then got on his hands and knees and crawled under the table. The magistrate's breath smelled so foul that he felt sick. He worked fast, pulling out a small dagger and cutting the leather tie that fastened the keychain to Bjorn's belt. The keys jangled when he stuck them under his cloak. That same instant someone seized his shoulder roughly and dragged him out from under the table.

"What are you doing, boy, moping around under there?! You weren't eavesdropping, were you?" asked Thorkell harshly. "Get yourself to bed!"

"No sir, I mean yes…yes, sir," the boy stammered, staring at the floor and crossing his arms tightly over his chest. Had Father Thorkell seen the keys, it would have been all over. Michael glanced up at his mother. Her expression was stern, and his head sank even lower. "I'll be off, then; God give you a good night," he mumbled into his chest and rushed out before they could answer, half-running out of the hall and down the corridor.

The calm autumn night was dark and freezing. He wished he'd put on a better overcoat. His cloak reached only just below his groin, and there was little warmth in his tight breeches. But he had to be quick; his mother was just as likely to check on him soon in the bed that had been made for them. Michael put his head down and shuffled into the icy breeze blowing across the field to the east of the farmhouses, toward the storehouse that was attached to the stable. Frost was beginning to form, and the brittle grass crunched beneath his feet. He kept his head lowered in the dark and did not see the guard by the storehouse wall before he almost bumped into him. Of course someone had been positioned to guard the prisoners; what an idiot not to have thought of that! Now what? How would he explain his presence there? The man was one of the Enni domestics, a short, stout, middle-aged man, with broad shoulders and an almost square face, his forehead and chin almost equally wide.

"What is your business here? Surely they haven't sent a young lad to replace me?" he grumbled. "My shift was supposed to end at nightfall, and the godforsaken Englishmen all fell asleep ages ago. I'm freezing my rump out here."

"Ehm…no," Michael answered uncertainly, "or, well…yes, sort of." He suddenly had an idea and launched into an explanation, speaking rapidly. "All evening they've been gorging themselves on meat and gulping down mead in the warmth inside. No one wants to come out, so I was sent to tell you to go inside and eat something before it's all gone."

"No one wants to come out?!" The man looked at him, indignant and slightly suspicious. "What the hell…?!"

Michael shrugged. "They're all dead drunk. And it's awful cold."

"Morons! And here I am freezing to death while they sit in there drinking and having a grand old time!"

Michael cocked his head. "I could stay out here for a while, just while you go in and warm up a bit and have something to eat."

The man looked doubtful. "That will hardly work. You're just a kid. What if the villains try to escape?"

"Didn't you just say they were sound asleep? And anyway, how will they get out?"

He pointed to the bolt and the big lock in the latch of the storehouse door. "They can't break a bolt *and* a hanging lock from the inside. If I hear anything, I'll run to the farm right away and call for help."

"Hmm. Maybe that's not such a bad idea, boy." The servant gave it some thought. After all, he was cold and desperately hungry. "All right." He wrinkled his forehead. "Weren't you at Holl yesterday and didn't you see…?" He didn't finish the sentence. Michael concurred in a low voice and looked at his toes.

"You've got spunk, kid," he said, looking at the boy with admiration and patting him on the head. Then he turned and walked swiftly up the field. "I won't be long. Or if I am, I'll send someone out," he called over his shoulder.

"Take your time," Michael called back and waved. No one had ever praised his courage before. He almost felt ashamed of what he was about to do to the guard. But maybe no one would notice a single prisoner missing in the morning.

As soon as the servant was out of sight, he put his ear to a small knothole in the storeroom door. They were asleep—no question. Amazing how loud their snoring was. He put his mouth to the knothole and called Oswald Miller's name as loudly as he dared.

No answer.

"Oswald Miller!"

Still no answer, but someone had woken up. The snoring became less audible, and he could hear movement inside.

"Who's there?" someone asked suddenly in English, and Michael sighed with relief. He knew that gruff voice.

"It's me, Michael!"

A brown, bloodshot eye looked out through the knothole. "Is that you, kid? Praise the Lord! I knew I could rely on you, my young friend!" Oswald's voice was almost weepy.

"Yes," said Michael, suddenly finding it hard to speak. He leaned his forehead against the door and gnashed his teeth. Was he doing the right thing? Could he be absolutely sure that Oswald hadn't done anything to Einhildur? He hadn't heard him, but then again he'd covered his ears the whole time. How could he be sure?

"Michael?"

"I'm here."

"You know I wasn't involved in what happened there at the farm, Michael." Oswald spoke quickly. "I couldn't stop them— they were like animals, just mad. And now they've been executed for their sins, decapitated and buried like the beasts they were."

The boy swallowed and wiped his nose with the back of his hand.

"I'm going to open the door, Oswald," he said softly. "I have the keys. But you have to promise to come out alone. I don't want to let anyone out but you. And you have to be quick because the guard will be back soon, and I have to put the bolt back and lock the door so he doesn't notice anything."

"I give you my word," said Oswald solemnly. "Now hurry up and open the door."

Michael examined the keys on the chain. They were all similar in make and size and impossible to see which one fit the hanging lock. There was nothing to do but try them all, one by one. On the fourth try, he heard a faint click and the lock opened. Yet the race was not yet won, even if the lock was out of the latch that kept the bolt in place. He now had to force the heavy wooden bolt out of the iron holders on each side of the door. That was easier said than done. He was barely able to lift the bolt and needed to use all his strength to force it out of the holder on one side. Still, that was not good enough; the bolt needed to be lifted out of both holders at the same time. Michael let it drop and wiped the sweat from his forehead, nervous and shaking: surely the guard would be back at any moment.

"Push on the goddamn bolt, boy! Push it to one side," a voice thundered on the other side of the door. Yes, of course, why hadn't he thought of that? Michael spit into his palms and pushed on the end of the bolt with all his might. Slowly but surely it slipped out of the holders and dropped to the ground with a low thud.

Instantly the door was thrown open and the Englishmen rushed out, shadows in the dark, whispering to each other. Someone laughed softly at the naïveté of this stupid boy and seized hold of his shoulder when he was about to run away; it was captain Bell. Michael yelled and protested loudly, calling to his friend in despair: "You promised, Oswald Miller!" He thrashed and kicked; the toe of his boot hit a soft groin, and its owner cursed loudly. Michael felt a heavy blow to the back of his neck, and then everything went black.

⟨❖⟩

The magistrate's keychain could not be found, so the hanging lock had to be demolished. It was already past daybreak when someone decided it might be an idea to check on the prisoners and toss some food their way. Major chaos ensued when Michael's childish voice was heard, calling for help from inside the store-room. Soon a small crowd had gathered outside the door. The servant who had been deployed to guard the storeroom the night before was found bound and gagged inside the stable, carefully concealed beneath a mound of hay.

Thorkell stood impatiently over the servants as they tried with shaking hands to open the lock with a chisel. When those attempts failed, he grabbed a sledgehammer, pushed them aside, and smashed the lock in one fell swoop. He forced the bolt out of the iron holders with one movement, cast it aside, and threw open the heavy door. Ragna pushed her way through the people who stood watching and rushed after him into the darkened, windowless storehouse, calling out for her son.

A quiet sniffling could be heard from the furthest corner. Michael lay there curled up in a low shakedown beneath a woolen cover, his hands and feet tied. He had been calling for help since regaining consciousness during the night, and he was exhausted, his face swollen from crying. His teeth chattered from the cold. Ragna ran to him and cut the ropes with her knife, took her son in her arms, and stroked his hair. "What happened, my darling? What on earth happened?!" He had received a cut from the blow to his head, and the hair at the back of his neck was moist and sticky. Ragna cried out as she felt the blood on her palm. Michael stammered, trying to respond; then suddenly Thorkell was there. He shoved Ragna aside, seized the boy's shoulders, and shook him roughly.

"What the hell have you done, you miserable wretch?! Why did you release them?!"

"We don't know if it was him who opened the door or someone else, Thorkell," Ragna said angrily. "He can barely lift the bolt, and anyway, why would he do something like that? Can't you see they've hurt him and tied him up?! Thank God he hasn't died of exposure!"

"Of course it was him who let them out. Who else but this worthless English bastard!" Thorkell raised the boy to his feet and shook him again. "Admit it, you lout!"

Michael nodded his head rapidly, too frightened to speak.

Thorkell released his shoulders and shoved him away, full of contempt, and the boy nearly fell backward. "I knew it."

Ragna grasped her son's hands. "Why, Michael?!"

He reeled, still unsteady, his feet numb from the ropes. "Mamma," he said, his voice hoarse. "Mamma, I...I only wanted to open the door for Oswald. He was my friend. My only friend."

Thorkell was livid with rage. The veins on his temples and neck looked about to burst, and his narrow face was inflamed. Ragna had never seen him like that. "Your friend?!" he hissed. "I'll teach you how to be friends with those English mongrels!" There was a loud slap as he hit the boy across the face with his open palm, first once, then again, and again, and again. Michael howled in pain and fell to the floor crying, holding his burning cheeks. Ragna grabbed Thorkell's arm and tried to drag him away from the boy, but to no avail. Horrified, she watched as he dragged Michael to his feet by the hair and hit him again, this time with a closed fist so that he was propelled across the floor. Michael lay motionless where he had fallen, blood streaming from his nose.

"Thorkell, stop it!" she shouted, on the verge of tears. "What's gotten into you?! You're not yourself! Are you mad?"

He turned to face her, his eyes black with rage. "Do not accuse me of madness, you harlot! Don't you understand what your bastard has done to me?!" He lowered his voice and narrowed his eyes, taking a step in her direction. "Or perhaps you do understand. I wouldn't put it past you to have planned this whole thing and handed him the keys. You whore! Don't think I don't know why you were so loath to follow me from Holar!"

Ragna took a step backward, shocked. "What are you talking about? How can you say such things?"

He took hold of her upper arm and pulled her to him roughly. "I saw often enough how he ogled you, that English swine, and now they say that he is calling you his cousin. Imagine! Cousin to an English bishop! Everyone knows what that means. You've lain under an Englishman before, and don't pretend you didn't enjoy it."

Finally it dawned on her what he was accusing her of. All at once her pain, anguish, jealousy about Gudrun, and accumulated rage bubbled to the surface like a geyser about to erupt. A manic scream rang out, and somewhere in the distance she recognized that it was she who screamed. The knife she had used to cut Michael's fetters was still in her hand, and almost as though it had a mind of its own, her hand rose into the air and the sharp knife headed straight for Thorkell's heart. He dodged the blow, lashed out at her, and suddenly the knife was in his hand. Her wrist was throbbing from where he had hit her, but she refused to let him get away and leapt at him again, reaching for the knife. In the same instant, she tripped and fell forward. The knife blade grazed her breast and she felt a burning sting. That same moment more people came into the storeroom, shouting about what was going on and asking what had happened to the Englishmen.

Thorkell tossed the knife into a corner and told the people in a harsh voice to leave. It was vital now, he said, for all able-bodied men to ride to Holar as soon as possible; the villains had escaped while they were sleeping off their drunken stupor.

A few people made a move to attend to Ragna, who lay doubled up on the dirty floor, clutching her chest. Her breath was labored, and she made hollow sucking noises as though she might suffocate. But Thorkell ordered everyone out and accepted no protests. The door was shut and darkness surrounded Ragna and Michael, save for a small ray of light that shone in through a knothole in the door panel. A scraping sound could be heard on the other side as the bolt was dragged across the door. Thorkell's deep voice forbade anyone from opening it. "The woman is hysterical. She's a danger to herself and others."

With difficulty, Ragna rose up on all fours and crawled over to Michael, who was lying motionless on the floor. She could barely see the outlines of objects in the storeroom, but as her eyes adjusted to the dark, she saw that he was conscious and holding his nose to stop the bleeding.

"Mamma, I'm sorry," he whispered desolately. "I only wanted to let Oswald go because he saw me at Holl and spared my life."

She did not answer, just removed her shawl and wrapped it around him, tucking the ends beneath his arms. She shivered; she only had on a thin woven dress, and the storeroom was freezing. Judging by the stifling odor, the magistrate's makeshift prison had not been cleaned in a long while.

"Dearest, you're so cold," she said. "You must have been terrified out here all night in the cold and dark."

"Just a little," he admitted so softly that it was almost inaudible. He was on the verge of tears. She stroked his cheek gently.

"I should be the one asking for your forgiveness, my darling boy."

"Why?" he asked, surprised. She sighed deeply. What could she tell him? How could he understand her actions at his young age?

"I put all my faith in Father Thorkell," she said quietly. "I thought it would be best for us both to follow him. He was kind to me last winter."

Outside there was a clamor of shouting and stomping hooves. The men were leaving.

"Do you love him, even when he talks to you like that?"

Ragna was silent for a long while before answering. "I…don't know anymore," she finally said. "I think…" She shook her head, confused. "It's almost like he's possessed by a dark power."

Michael sat up and took his hand from his nose. The bleeding had stopped. "It's so cold."

Ragna stood up, reeling slightly, and fumbled her way to the door in the dark. She peered out through the knothole. There were a few women standing in a cluster a short distance away, talking.

"Help!" Ragna shouted, banging on the storeroom door with her palm. "Open the door!"

The women glanced uncertainly toward the storeroom.

"Please open it, in God's name!"

One of the women broke from the group and strode toward the storeroom door. It was Thorunn, the magistrate's wife, a tall, vigorous woman. "Don't just stand there like nervous chickens!" she called over her shoulder. "I may be strong, but I can't lift the bolt by myself!"

A moment later the door was open and they were free. The women exclaimed in alarm when Ragna and Michael stepped out into the daylight. Ragna held her torn and bloody dress against her chest with a flat palm, drops of blood seeping out between her fingers. The gash reached from her collarbone down to her breast. The boy's face was swollen, and his clothes were covered with dried blood, though clearly from a nosebleed, since there was a line of blood from his nose down to his chin.

"Help her, she's about to fall!" Ragna heard the words as though from a distance. Her feet refused to obey, and then the world swirled before her eyes.

"No doubt they have run straight to the bishop and are now hiding under his robe. And it's just as certain that Craxton will believe all their distortions and lies," Thorkell had told the men as they rode along Hjaltadalur Valley. Yet even he was taken aback when he saw the bishop's men, both English and Icelandic, awaiting their arrival. They had formed a semicircle around St. Mary's Cathedral and were armed and ready for battle. In the steeple windows, there were archers at the ready with their bows drawn and arrow tips gleaming. The villains themselves were nowhere in sight; it was obvious where they were keeping themselves. Just as obvious was the fact that the new arrivals were up against a force of superior strength, even though the bishop's men were outnumbered. Craxton stood in full regalia on the stone pavement in front of the cathedral doors, his feet apart, arms crossed, stone-gray eyes glaring at them from under heavy brows. The battle was effectively over before it had begun. Bjorn the magistrate leaned toward Thorkell, remarking that it was useless to pursue the matter any further; it would be best for them to turn around before any harsh words were exchanged with Bishop Craxton. He spoke on behalf of those among them who cowered at the thought of the bishop's power to excommunicate them, who feared the same the fate as Father Jon Palsson and who now wondered how they'd allowed themselves to be persuaded to take part in this fool's errand in the first place.

Thorkell ignored him. Dismounting, he took long strides up to the church step, only stopping when two of the bishop's men crossed their spears in front of him, halting his approach.

He put out his hands with his palms turned upward so they could see that he was unarmed. He fixed his gaze on Craxton. "Are you forbidding a servant of God from entering His house? Do you forget that it is grounds for excommunication to assault an ordained man?!"

The men hesitated and looked at one another, then glanced at the bishop. Father Thorkell had been their superior until just recently.

"It seems to me that you yourself have forgotten the role of an ordained man," answered Craxton coldly. "It is a decidedly more serious offense to violate the sanctity of the church and the home of one's bishop than to defend him when he is attacked. You said so yourself only a few months ago. Or why are you here in the company of armed men?"

"The bishop may be unaware that his countrymen, who now shelter themselves beyond the altar rails, are known to be robbers and murderers. They defile the house of God with their presence," Thorkell replied. "Our business is with them, not our bishop. Our only wish is that the violators be turned over to the king's magistrate so that they may be tried and sentenced according to the law of God and the land."

The bishop shook his head. "They have been offered the sanctity and freedom of the holy church. The inviolability of the church will not be broken."

"I would not have taken Your Grace for the protector of rapists and child murderers," said Thorkell. "Or on what grounds does the bishop justify pardoning the slaying of an infant, the grandson of Lawman Thorsteinn Olafsson, as well as the elderly parents-in-law of his only daughter?"

"Was the child the lawman's grandson?" Craxton was visibly shaken, but he quickly regained his composure. "The sailors have told me that the guilty agents, four men, were tried and executed yesterday. They also said that five others from their ranks were fatally wounded in a merciless attack as they lay sleeping and oblivious."

Thorkell cried out in protest, but Craxton put up his hand, signaling for him to keep quiet; he had not finished. He continued, authoritatively: "The holy church of Holar will do all it can to prevent further bloodshed. Last fall, the Holar see purchased half a stake in the vessel *Bartholomew*, and now the captain and vessel owner have turned over their full share to Holar cathedral. Consequently, those who so much as touch the ship or its cargo receive major excommunication, as will those who threaten the lives and limbs of the men who now enjoy the protection of the church. If you wish to keep your position and your cloak, Father Thorkell, I would advise you to stop now and leave this place."

Thorkell stared at John Williamsson Craxton. The bishop's words crashed over him like an ice-cold wave. Everything he had worked for was in ruins. The dream that had driven him these five long years was dissolving in the cold frost of the morning, and the throbbing pain in his head and chest had him gasping for air. He had wagered everything and lost. Why had it all gone wrong? He reeled, could not think straight, yet knew that he must say something, if only to retain his dignity and gain some sort of resolution. But no words escaped his lips.

"Thorkell?" Someone touched his shoulder. He turned in a flash, ready to strike. Bjorn the magistrate recoiled as he looked into Thorkell's eyes. There was madness in them.

<figure><❖></figure>

The gash was not as deep as it had seemed at first, in spite of all the bleeding. When her wound had been washed and dressed, Ragna requested that horses be saddled for her and Michael. Thorunn, the magistrate's wife, protested loudly; Ragna needed to rest and recover from her injury, and her boy slept so soundly that he almost seemed in a coma, poor thing, exhausted as he was from all the horrors of the last few days. But Ragna was adamant: she would go to Hjaltadalur on foot if no horse was available; after all, it wasn't such a great distance. She had to speak to Klaengur the Red today, before he left Holar for his ship. Tomorrow was Michaelmas, September 29, and *Christopher* of Hull would sail at daybreak. Thorunn shook her head with concern, but seeing that Ragna would not be dissuaded, she not only lent her horses but also ordered one of the two servants who had stayed behind at the farm to escort her.

They set off near midday. They rode slowly, both on account of the pack horse carrying their belongings, and also because the servant was keeping the promise he'd made to his mistress not to let Ragna take off at a trot, for fear that her wound might open up again. They had just passed the woods by Hrishals Pass when they saw a group of riders coming toward them. Ragna shouted to Michael and the servant to follow her, tapped her horse with her whip, and took off at a gallop down the path and into the forest, colorful leaves flying up from beneath the horse's hooves. They followed behind her, Michael pale with fear. She steered her horse away from the path into a thicket of tall, narrow birch trees. The servant was surprised and angry, and he demanded to know what she was thinking. She hushed him angrily. Did he not see that they needed to hide? Had he not seen that morning how Thorkell had hurt them and locked them in the storeroom? Fortunately the man clammed up, for a moment later, just as they were out of sight, they heard the clattering of hooves and the riders came into view.

Ragna watched them ride past, one after another, so close that she could smell the foulness of their breath and sweat. All the men had to do was glance to one side and they would see them beyond the leafless trees. But they looked neither right nor left, just sat hunched over on their horses: yesterday's victors were today's defeated. Thorkell brought up the rear, riding a short distance behind the others. The cold wind tore at his black cloak so that it blew up and flapped back from his shoulders in a straight line, like a raven's wings. He sat upright in the saddle and looked straight ahead, yet it was almost as though he sensed them there, for when he approached, he slowed his horse and peered in among the trees. For one brief moment, his eyes met Ragna's and held them. Then he passed and did not look back.

◈

"Did Father Thorkell try to force you…into intercourse?"

Ragna shook her head.

"Well, he must have—they found you all bruised and bleeding after he had been with you, and you and the boy nearly naked, standing in the storeroom in this cruel frost! He hurt you, you've said as much, and it's obvious to all."

"It was an accident," she said in a flat voice without looking up, and she inadvertently raised her hand to the bandage on her chest. "It's only a scratch. The fault is mine as much as his."

"She hardly seems like herself," a worried Craxton whispered to his scribe. "Could he have given her some sort of concoction he brewed?"

"To be sure," Jon Egilsson concurred softly. "Thorkell Gudbjartsson has long had a reputation for dabbling in the dark arts—more than other men. Some have even taken to calling him Thorkell Galdur of the Dark Arts."

"What was the man's purpose in taking you from this place with force?" The bishop was becoming irritated. "I am also told that he took a trunk and some packages belonging to you, without your consent."

"I was the one who took them," said Ragna abruptly.

Craxton looked at her in surprise. "Why?"

She hesitated. "From Enni," she said after a moment. "I took them with me from there."

The bishop leaned back in his chair and drummed the tips of his fingers lightly together, looking at her with an ambiguous expression. Did he suspect the truth? Well, they could think what they wanted. It didn't matter now.

"Write in the indictment, Jon, that Thorkell locked Ragna and her son inside a storeroom in a bitter frost, that he tried to force my cousin's hand and cut her with a knife so that she bled," said the bishop resolutely. "And also that he stole items belonging to her." The scribe hesitated a moment, then dipped a white swan's feather into his inkwell. He gave Ragna a questioning look, waiting for her protestations. But she said nothing, just stared at her hands in her lap, and they took her silence for agreement.

Quickly Jon wet the tip of the pen with his tongue and began to write.

◈

The ship skips on the raging waves, and the tackle and spar crackle as the icy autumn winds fill the sails. All around is the vast ocean. It has been a long time since we have seen other ships.

At first I was hopelessly seasick and could keep no nourishment down. I felt so ill in both my body and mind that had it not been for Michael's constant attention, I might not have been able to resist the temptation to throw myself overboard and disappear forever into the all-enclosing darkness. Such was my desire to flee the life that God would have me live. Such was my cowardice.

In a few days' time, we shall see the shores of Greenland, says Klaengur the Red. The land of my father and his people. Somewhere from the deep, the mother of the sea summons the Skraelings to comb her tangled hair and rewards them with an abundant catch.

I look at the blue horizon, where sea and sky merge into one, and think about all that has transpired. To my own great surprise, I no longer feel only emptiness and sadness. A tiny flame flutters deep in the darkness of my soul. I still long for something to call my own.

Maybe I was mad—spellbound. What other than his galdur could have held me in thrall? One day, Thorkell Gudbjartsson shall be erased from my heart like the footsteps in the sand that vanish beneath the gentle waves.

On that day I shall be free.

ABOUT THE AUTHOR

Photograph © Johann Pall Valdimarsson

Vilborg Davidsdottir earned a degree in media studies from the University of Iceland in 1991, a BA in folkloristics and English in 2005, and an MA in folkloristics in 2011. She worked in the media for fifteen years as a journalist, radio programmer, and TV reporter but has focused on her writing since 2000. She has written six novels, three of which—*By the Well of Fates* (1993), *The Norns Judgment* (1994), and *Audur* (2009)—take place during the Viking Age in Iceland, Scandinavia, Scotland, and Ireland. Her other three novels—*Sacrifice* (1997), *On the Cold Coasts* (2000), and *Raven* (2005)—are set in fourteenth- and fifteenth century Iceland and Greenland. *On the Cold Coasts* is her first book to be translated into English. Vilborg lives in Reykjavik with her husband and is the mother of three children, aged seven, seventeen, and twenty-four.

ABOUT THE TRANSLATOR

Photograph © Annie Atkins

Alda Sigmundsdottir is a writer, journalist, and translator. She grew up in Iceland, Canada, and Cyprus, and she has also lived in Great Britain and Germany. Her translation work spans almost two decades and includes everything from annual reports to literature. She chronicled Iceland's economic meltdown on her English-language blog, "The Iceland Weather Report," and she has subsequently been a frequent commentator and lecturer on her country's social and economic situation. She has also written extensively about Iceland for the foreign press. Her first book, *The Little Book of the Icelanders*, was recently published by Forlagid in Iceland. She lives in Reykjavik with her husband and daughter.